Young Christian's Pilgrimage

Young Christian's Pilgrimage

A Victorian Children's Story based on John Bunyan's
PILGRIM'S PROGRESS   Part 1

BRIDGE PUBLISHING, INC.
Publishers of
LOGOS • HAVEN • OPEN SCROLL

Other Children's Classics Revised and Updated by Christopher Wright:

Christiana's Journey by John Bunyan
Target Earth! by John Bunyan
Christie's Old Organ by Mrs. O.F. Walton
A Peep Behind the Scenes by Mrs. O.F. Walton
The Rocky Island and Other Stories
        by Samuel Wilberforce and Margaret Gatty
Mary Jones and Her Bible by M.E.R.
At the Back of the North Wind by Geo. MacDonald

Young Christian's Pilgrimage by John Bunyan
ISBN 0-88270-534-2
Copyright © 1982 this revised edition
        by Christopher Wright

Published by:
Bridge Publishing Inc.
2500 Hamilton Blvd.
South Plainfield, NJ 07080

Contents

John Bunyan's dream.

CHAPTER 1

Young Christian Hears
of the Heavenly City

Christian lived in a great city called Destruction. Its streets were full of boys and girls, laughing and playing all day long. This was in the summer time, when the sun was shining and the city looked bright and pleasant. On the rainy days in winter the children did not feel so happy, and they would sometimes be glad to sit down quietly and listen to stories.

Now and then a man or a woman with a kind face would come to the city for a short time, and these strangers always tried to make friends with the children, and were willing to tell them stories whenever they would listen.

"There is a beautiful country," they would say, "far away from this city. A very good and wise King rules over it. He cares for you children very much. The Prince to whom *your* city belongs is wicked and cruel, and he hates the good King. One day an army will come from the King's country to fight against your Prince, and this city will be burned, and all the people in it will be killed!"

Then the children asked, "What will become of us?"

And the strangers always answered, "You must leave this city now, while you are young and strong,

1

They laughed all the more.

and travel to the King's country. In the Heavenly City where He lives you will be safe."

Young Christian heard this many times, and he often thought about it; but whenever he said to his friends, "Shall we go to the Heavenly City?" they laughed at him, and told him that it was only a make-believe story about the King, and that no city could be better or safer than their own.

But Christian felt quite sure that the strangers had spoken the truth, and one day he found an old Book. In it were written the very same things about the King and the Heavenly City, and their own wicked Prince, and his city which would certainly be destroyed when the King came.

He showed the Book to his companions, but they laughed all the more, and said, "That Book was written so long ago that it is of no use now. The King's army has never come, and very likely it never will! At any rate we may as well play as long as we can."

But young Christian did not want to play. He felt unhappy, and sat down and wondered whether he could find the way to the Heavenly City by himself. He was afraid he might be lost if he tried to make the long journey alone. Opening his Book again, he read in it about the King's own Son, who had once visited the City of Destruction, and had spoken kindly to the people in the streets, saying, "Let the children come to me."

"If He were only here now," thought Christian, "perhaps He would take me back with Him; but I could

3

never go all that long, long way alone!"

Then he looked down and saw how soiled and dusty his clothes had become. He had worn them a long time, and he had played so much that they were getting quite thin and shabby. This added to his sadness, for he thought that if he *did* find his way to the Heavenly City, his clothes would be worn out long before he got there, and how could he expect the King to receive him dressed in nothing but rags?

At last he took up his Book and went home. Christian was lonely at home. His mother was dead, but his guardian asked him why he looked so tired and sad. Christian told her that he would like to go to the Heavenly City; but she laughed, as his friends had done, and said, "You are a foolish boy. There is no Heavenly City. If you go wandering along the roads after those strangers you will get lost."

So Christian went to bed and felt very miserable. It was a long time until he fell asleep.

CHAPTER 2

Christian Is Found by Evangelist

When Christian went out the next morning the sun was shining, and his companions were running about. They called to him to join them; but he said, "I cannot play. I think we all ought to start on our journey."

"What a stupid boy you are," they cried, "to be always talking about that Heavenly City! You had better go and look for it instead of staying here and spoiling our fun!"

So they ran away, and Christian stayed by himself.

Presently Christiana came down the street with her baby sister. She had been standing by when the boys had laughed at Christian the day before, and she had felt very sorry that he should be teased. Christian liked Christiana, and he was glad to see her coming.

She stopped to speak to him.

"You are upset again, Christian! You should not listen to what the strangers say if it makes you so unhappy. Come up the hill and help me look after the baby."

Christiana was gentle, and though she did not believe the stories he had told her out of his Book, she never laughed at him as the others did.

"You know," he said, as they walked along, "I *must*

go to the King, because I have a burden to carry, and no one but He can take it from me."

"Where is your burden?" asked Christiana.

"It is on my back, and it feels so heavy that it makes me too tired to play."

Christiana looked puzzled. "I think you must be ill, Christian, if you imagine such things. You haven't any burden on your back!"

"Ah," said the boy, "*you* cannot see it, but I can feel that it is there, and I shall always be tired until it is gone."

They climbed the hill and were happy together; but when Christian went home at night he began to think of the Heavenly City again. He had no mother to comfort him, and his father was one of the great men of the city, and had little time to spend with his son.

Christian hoped that he would meet Christiana again in the morning; but she was busy at home, and the other boys and girls would have nothing to do with him. So he wandered off into the fields by himself, and sat down upon a bank to think. After a while he heard a step coming near, and looking up he saw one of the strangers on his way to visit Christian's city; a man with a pleasant face, whose name was Evangelist. He had seen Christian before, and he turned aside to speak to him.

"Why are you so upset?" he asked, for there were signs of tears in Christian's eyes.

Christian felt so comforted by the sound of Evangelist's voice that he told him all his troubles at once. How he wished to obey the King, and how his friends had laughed at him, and how even his guardian and Christiana did not believe that the stories about the Heavenly City were true.

Then Evangelist spoke to him very wisely. "The stories are all quite true," he said. "The King loves everyone. If you will obey Him and begin your journey, He will watch over you all the way, and when you reach the Heavenly City you will be safe for ever."

"I would go now," said Christian, "if I only knew the way."

Evangelist turned round and looked across the fields, along the path by which he had come. "Do you see the Gate in the far distance?" and he pointed to it with his finger.

But young Christian's eyes were still dim with tears, so that he could not see the Gate.

"Well," said Evangelist, "there is a light shining above it. Can you see that?"

"Yes," said the boy, "I think I can."

"The way to the Heavenly City is through that Gate. It is called the Gate to the King's Way. It is like a large door set in the wall. You must go through the door to begin your journey. There is no other way to start. The King's Son made that door. Now I will give you a message from the King. It is a promise from the King to all travelers."

Evanglist drew out a paper, which he put into Christian's hand. There were words written upon it by the King's Son Himself in gold and beautiful colours, and Christian read them aloud:—

"I AM THE WAY, THE TRUTH, AND
THE LIFE. NO ONE GOES TO THE
FATHER EXCEPT BY ME."

Evangelist smiled. "Now, if you wish to meet the
King, do not be upset any more, but go quickly to that
Gate and knock. One of the King's servants will open
it, and he will tell you where to go next. You have only
to knock, and the door will be opened!"

CHAPTER 3

Obstinate and Pliable

Some boys were playing near the city, and they saw Evangelist speaking to Christian. They were not surprised at this, because they knew that the strangers who said they were from the Heavenly City always talked to the children; but when Evangelist turned away, and Christian began to run across the fields towards the Gate, they all wondered where he was going.

"Christian is running away!" cried one.

"He must be going to look for that Heavenly City!" said another.

"Then he will be lost!" exclaimed a third.

"We ought to go after him and bring him back."

There were two boys named Obstinate and Pliable, who knew Christian very well. They were older than he was, but the three had often played together. Obstinate was not a pleasant companion, for he loved to have his own way, and Pliable used to give in to him for the sake of peace. Young Christian did not care much for either of them, but he liked Pliable better. How well their names suited them, he thought— difficult, and easily led!

These two boys were worried when they saw

Young Christian's Pilgrimage

Christian running alone over the fields, for although they were often cross and disagreeable to him, they did not like to think of him getting lost.

"We must make him come back," said Obstinate. "What a stupid boy he is to believe everything he is told!"

"Come along, then," said Pliable, "I will go with you."

So the two boys set off, and as they ran they shouted to Christian to wait for them.

But Christian was frightened when he heard their voices, and would not even look round.

"If they take me back," he thought, "perhaps I may never be able to get away again."

He ran as fast as he could, but he soon began to feel tired because of the burden upon his back, and Obstinate and Pliable were taller and stronger than he was, so before long they caught up with him.

"Where are you going?" cried Obstinate. "What do you mean by making us run after you in this way!"

"I am going to the King's City," said Christian. "Won't you come with me?"

Obstinate laughed. "I should think not! What would be the good, when we are as happy as possible at home!"

"We should be a great deal happier with the King. His City is more beautiful than this, and we shall be quite safe there. I have told you before that our own city is not a safe place."

"As if you knew anything about it!" said Obstinate.

Obstinate and Pliable

"Why do you talk such nonsense?"

"It is not nonsense. It is written in my Book."

Then Obstinate laughed again. "How many times am I to tell you that your Book is full of rubbish? There is not one word of it true. Now are you coming back or not?"

Obstinate looked very cross, and young Christian's heart began to beat faster and faster, but he answered loudly, "No. I am going to the King!"

"Well, you may go, then," said Obstinate. "Come, Pliable, we might have saved ourselves the trouble of running after such a foolish boy. He doesn't know when he is well off!"

But Pliable stood still. "Don't you laugh at him," he said. "Just supposing the Book *is* true: he will be better off than we are. I think I shall go too."

"Oh yes, please come with me!" cried Christian. "You do not know how happy we shall be when we are living with the King."

"Are you *sure* you can find the City?" asked Pliable.

"Yes, for Evangelist told me what to do. We must go to that Gate in the distance there, and a man will show us the way."

"You don't mean to say you are going?" said Obstinate. "Why even if there were a Heavenly City, two boys like you could never find it!"

Pliable did not answer, but he made a few steps forward by the side of Christian. He had often listened to the words of the strangers, and he thought, "I may as well go as far as the Gate, and see what the road is like."

11

Young Christian's Pilgrimage

"I'm not surprised at Christian," continued Obstinate, "but really, Pliable, you ought to have more sense. Just come back with me, and I'll not tell anyone that you said you were going."

But Pliable was not very fond of Obstinate, and he felt pleased at the idea of having his own way; so he answered, "It's no use talking. I've made up my mind. Good-bye, if you won't come too."

"No, thank you! I'm glad enough to get rid of you both!" And with a mocking smile on his face, Obstinate turned back towards the City of Destruction.

CHAPTER 4

The Slough of Despair

"Now," said Pliable, when the two boys were left alone, "tell me what sort of a place this Heavenly City is."

"It is very beautiful," replied Christian. "Have you not heard the strangers talk about it? The King lives there, and His people never feel tired or unhappy. They wear shining clothes which can never fade and never grow old."

"I don't suppose they will let *us* in."

"Oh yes, they will; Evangelist said so! See, he gave me this," and Christian unfolded the King's message, and let Pliable read the words for himself. "The King sent that to me, to let me know He would like me to go to His City."

"He hasn't sent *me* one."

"You didn't meet Evangelist. But never mind, I am *sure* the King will be pleased to see you."

"Well, tell me something else. What will you do when you get to the City?"

"First of all I should like to see the King, and if He is very kind I shall ask him where my mother is. You know she went away when I was younger, and sometimes I have wanted her so much. One of the

Young Christian's Pilgrimage

strangers told me that she was with the King, so I think she must be living in the Heavenly City."

"I wonder how long it will take us to get there. Did you ask Evangelist? We might walk a little faster, I think."

"I wish I could!" sighed Christian, who was tired already. "I'm afraid I shall be very slow on the way. It is this burden, which is so heavy that at times I can hardly walk."

Pliable was just going to say, "What do you mean by always pretending that you have a burden to carry?" when suddenly his feet sank deep into the grass, and he saw that he had walked into a marsh, or slough. "Oh!" cried he, "where are we now?"

"I don't know," said poor Christian, whose burden made him sink deeper than Pliable into the soft, green mud. "Let us try to get out."

But the boys were frightened and confused, and they could not tell which was the way out of the marsh. It was called the Slough of Despair, and it was a dangerous place even for grown-up people. Every step the children took seemed to lead them further into it, and at last Pliable grew very angry.

"See what a mess we are in!" said he; "and it is all your fault! I wish I had not come. If this is the beginning of our journey, what else may we expect on the road? Just let me get out of this horrible marsh and I shall go straight home again. You may look for the City by yourself!"

Christian did not answer, for he was too frightened

Pliable at last succeeded.

and upset to speak. His clothes were covered with mud, and every moment he feared that he would be smothered in the Slough. How he wished that Evangelist would come to help him, but he could not see any one near to him. Far away, across the fields, shone the light above the Gate to the King's Way, and behind him lay the City of Destruction. Pliable turned away from the light, and at last succeeded in getting out of the marsh; but he never stopped to help his companion, and when Christian looked back he saw Pliable running home as fast as he could. How desolate Christian felt when Pliable was out of sight!

"But I *will* go to the King!" he said, and once more he struggled on, trying to find some firm ground. Then, when he had almost given up, he heard a voice saying, "Wait, I am coming to help you!"

CHAPTER 5

Help Finds Christian

Christian looked around when he heard the voice. He had made up his mind that Evangelist was wrong, and that the King did not want children travelling along the road to His beautiful City.

"I am young," he thought, "and so stupid! I cannot even get safely across these fields, and what should I do if I came to a high mountain or a deep river?"

The voice belonged to a boy named Help, who was one of the King's servants. He had noticed poor Christian struggling in the Slough. Help was a kind-hearted boy, and he ran at once to see what he could do.

"How did you fall in?" he asked; and Christian told him what had happened.

"Evangelist said I was to go to the Gate, and I did not know about this marsh."

"Didn't you see the stepping-stones?"

"No, I was talking to Pliable, and we were not looking at the ground."

"That was foolish. Where is Pliable?"

"He got out; but he went home, and did not try to help me."

"Well, don't be frightened; I shall be able to reach you in a minute. The King will always take care of you.

"Put your foot here."

Help Finds Christian

I wondered why He sent me over the fields today, but it was because He knew you would need me. Take hold of my hand and put your foot here. See! You are quite safe."

Christian stood trembling with fright, hardly believing he was safe.

"You are very kind," he said. "I could never have got out by myself."

"No," replied Help, "I don't think you could. Are you going to the Heavenly City?"

"I wish to go, but I am afraid the way will be too hard for me. Perhaps I had better wait until I am older."

"No, you must not wait. The King will watch over you, and whenever you need a friend to help you He will send somebody."

"Are you sure?" asked Christian. "I am young and the others all said I was stupid."

"Never mind what people say. When you are one of the King's pilgrims you will be quite safe. You may find the road long and hard, but if you keep on bravely you will come to the City at last, and then you will forget your trouble, because you will be so glad to see the King."

Help spoke so kindly that Christian did not feel afraid of talking to him.

"Do you think I shall find my mother in the Heavenly City?" he said. "She is with the King."

"If she is with the King you will find her. Is it long since she went away?"

"She went when I was little. I can remember her, and

Young Christian's Pilgrimage

we have her picture at home, so I shall be sure to know her."

"Then I have no doubt the King has told her already that you are coming to the City, and she will be watching for you," said Help.

Help had been kneeling on the ground, wiping the mud from Christian's clothes with tufts of grass. He rose now, saying, "You have soiled your clothes very much, but you will have new ones before you get to the City. Don't lose sight of the light over the Gate, and walk as quickly as you can until you reach it. Good-bye, and remember the King will take care of you."

"Just tell me one thing," said Christian. "Have you been to the City yourself?"

"No. I have been very nearly to its gates, and then the King gave me some work to do for Him, and I shall not go to live in the City until it is finished."

"How long will it take me to get there?"

"I cannot tell you that. For some people the journey is longer than for others. But if you love and obey the King, He will be sure to guide you to the City at the right time. Now I must go. If you are frightened again, call to the King, and He will hear you."

CHAPTER 6

Christian Meets With Worldly

Not very far from the City of Destruction there was a hill, and beyond the hill a village. In this village lived a number of people who called themselves the King's servants, and pretended to love and obey Him, although they did not really care about anything but their own pleasure and safety. They had been afraid to stay in the city, because of all that the strangers had told them, but they did not wish to take the trouble of going to the King's country. So they built houses and made fields and gardens for themselves beyond the hill, and fancied that in that place they were quite safe.

A boy from the village, whose name was Worldly, happened to be walking across the fields on the very day that young Christian began his journey. Worldly knew Christian by sight, because the people from the village often went into the City of Destruction to visit their old friends; and when he saw Christian coming, he wondered what he was doing so far from home.

"Is it you, Christian?" he asked. "You are a long way from your city."

Worldly was a tall, fine-looking boy, and Christian felt pleased to be noticed by him, so he answered at once, "I am going to the Gate to the King's Way."

Young Christian's Pilgrimage

"The Gate! What for?"

"To get rid of my burden."

"Oh, of course," replied Worldly. "I know those burdens are tiresome things. It isn't everybody who can feel them; but when you do feel them there is no comfort for you till they are gone."

Christian was surprised to hear Worldly speak in this way, for the boys and girls in his city had all laughed at him, and had declared that his burden was only his imagination. "With a name like his," thought Christian, "Worldly should know more about the world than the Heavenly City!"

"I hope I shall not have to carry it very much longer," Christian said out loud. "I am making haste to the Gate."

"Who put it into your head to go there?" asked Worldly.

"I met a man named Evangelist, and he told me to go."

Worldly laughed. "He may be very kind, but he is very stupid. I know him quite well. Look here, Christian, I can tell you a much better way of losing your burden. Don't you trouble to go all that long journey. Yes, you see, I know exactly what Evangelist said to you. He tells everyone the same thing. You have been in that horrid Slough already, and if you go through the Gate you will find worse troubles than that. There are wild beasts and all sorts of dangers, and very likely you will just die of hunger and tiredness."

"But my burden is *so* heavy," sighed Christian. "I

22

Christian Meets With Worldly

must get rid of it, and Evangelist said that was the *only* way."

"Well, of course you can do as you like," replied Worldly; "but I think you are very silly. How did you ever know that you had a burden at all?"

"I read in the King's Book that everyone has a burden."

"I thought so. That Book is all very well for clever, grown-up people, but boys like you can't understand it. You read it, and you don't know what it means, and you just get your head full of nonsense. Now, I'll tell you what to do. I wouldn't go back to your city, because you will always feel frightened, and it really isn't a very nice place to live in. If I were you, I should go round the hill to the village. I've some friends living in the first house you come to, and if you tell them that I sent you, they will take you in, and be as kind as possible. Then in a few days you'll forget all about your burden, and I don't suppose you will ever feel it again."

Christian felt puzzled. Worldly spoke so confidently that he could scarcely help believing what he said, and he thought it would be very nice to live near to his old home, and be able to see Christiana and his other friends sometimes.

"You can't do better than to take my advice," continued Worldly. "Never mind Evangelist. That is the way, past the hill. You can't mistake the house, because it is the first you come to."

Then he put his hands in his pockets and walked off, whistling a merry tune; and Christian forgot all about the King and His message, and turned away from the Gate to go to the village beyond the hill.

CHAPTER 7

The Wrong Path

Christian went on towards the village as quickly as he could, but he soon became very tired indeed. His burden seemed to grow heavier every minute, until at last he felt ready to fall down beneath its weight. By the time he reached the hill he could scarcely walk, and he wondered whether he would ever be able to get to the house in which the friends of young Worldly lived.

But when he turned the corner of the road which led round the hill, he almost forgot his burden, for he had never before seen anything so terrible as that path. The side of the hill was very rugged, and the rocks hung over the road, and looked just ready to fall.

Christian went a little way, but he was soon so frightened that he dared not take another step. He fancied he could see lightning and flames of fire darting out between the rocks, and he shook all over with fear.

"Oh, I wish I had not come!" he cried out. "What *shall* I do?"

Presently a man appeared at a little distance, and as he came nearer, Christian saw that it was Evangelist. He had no smile on his face, and poor Christian felt so ashamed and miserable that he almost wished the rocks *would* fall, and hide him from the sight of the friend whom he had disobeyed!

"What are you doing here?" asked Evangelist. But Christian hung down his head, and did not speak. "Are you not the boy whom I found outside the City of Destruction?"

"Yes," said Christian very quietly.

"Did I not show you the way to the Gate?"

"Yes."

"Then how is it you are here, for this is not the way to the Gate?"

"Oh," cried Christian, "I did not mean to do wrong, but I met a boy who told me I could get rid of my burden in the village; and I was so tired I thought I would come; but I am sure the hill will fall on me, and I am *so* frightened!"

Then Evangelist said in a kind voice, "Listen to me. The King sent me to tell you about the Heavenly City, and you had His promise that He would love you and watch over you. When you fell into the Slough of Despair, you know He sent Help to pull you out, and you have read in your Book that the King will always take care of those who trust in Him. Why did you believe what young Worldly said, and turn away from the right path?"

Poor Christian was now extremely upset, and Evangelist laid his hand gently on the boy's head.

"You have grieved the King," he said; "but if you are sorry He will forgive you."

"I will never disobey Him again," cried Christian. "I

"I will go with you past this hill."

am very, very sorry indeed: but are you sure that the King *will* forgive me?"

"Yes, the King will always forgive you, because of His Son, who loves all children."

"And may I still go to the Gate, or will the man there turn me away?"

"The King does not allow anyone to be turned away. You have only to knock, and he will open the Gate for you at once. Take my hand, and I will go with you past this hill."

Christian was very glad to put his hand in Evangelist's and be led back into the fields. The hill, with its terrible overhanging rocks, was soon left behind, and the light above the Gate could be clearly seen again.

"If you make haste," said Evangelist, "you will reach the Gate before it is dark, and you can stay there and rest until morning."

Then with a smile he bade the boy good-bye, and Christian started once more on his journey.

CHAPTER 8

Christian Enters the Gate

The sun was just setting when Christian reached the Gate to the King's Way. He had walked very quickly, for he did not wish to be in the fields after the darkness came on, and he was now so tired that he felt very glad indeed to see the Gate quite close to him.

It stood in a beautiful stone archway, and over it hung a lamp, which burned so brightly that its light could be seen even when the sun was shining. Round the top of the arch some words were carved by the King's Son upon the stone, and Christian stopped to read them. He read—

"KNOCK, AND THE DOOR WILL BE
OPENED TO YOU."

"That was what Evangelist said," thought Christian, and he began to knock upon the door. He listened, but he could not hear anyone coming, so he knocked again, and in a few minutes the door was opened by a man who looked something like Evangelist. He wore the same kind of long robe, and his face was kind. He smiled when he saw Christian, and said—

"Who is this at the Gate?"

"My name is Christian," replied the boy. "May I

come in?"

"Are you come from the City of Destruction?" asked the man, whose name was Goodwill.

"Yes, and I wish to go to the King."

Then Goodwill opened the Gate wide, and took Christian by the hand. As he was stepping in, Goodwill gave him a sudden pull.

"Why did you do that?" asked Christian in surprise.

Goodwill answered: "The Wicked Prince has a castle very near to this Gate, and sometimes when he sees anyone leaving his country, and entering the Way of the King, he commands his soldiers to shoot arrows at them."

Christian looked out, and saw the arrows lying upon the ground, and he felt very relieved to see Goodwill close the door firmly.

"Now I am safe," he thought.

Goodwill led him into his own house, which was just beyond the Gate, and made him sit down to rest while he prepared some food for him.

"Who told you the way to the Gate?" he asked.

"Evangelist," replied Christian; "and he said you would tell me where I have to go next."

"Yes, I will tell you. But how is it that you came alone? Have you no father or mother?"

"My mother is already with the King, and my father has so much to do that he cannot spare time for a journey, so I was obliged to come by myself."

"If your mother is with the King, she must have passed through this Gate. No doubt you will hear of her as you go on your way."

"Do you think I shall?" asked Christian eagerly, for the greatest wish he had at this moment was to know something more of his mother. "Help said that the King would tell her I was coming, and she would look out for me. Is that true?"

"Quite true. You will not see her until you reach the Heavenly City, but perhaps she will sometimes be able to see you. Have you come straight from home? Did not your friends try to persuade you to stay with them?"

"Obstinate and Pliable came after me, and Obstinate was angry; but Pliable said he would like to go to the Heavenly City. Then we fell into the Slough of Despair, and he was frightened, so he went back again. I thought I should never get out, but Help came, and he was very good to me."

"And what then?"

Christian felt his face turn red. "I was as bad as Pliable," he said, "for when I met Worldly I listened to him, and went towards the village. The road is so dreadful, and I was afraid the rocks would crush me; but Evangelist found me, and brought me into the fields again."

Goodwill smiled. "Well, now you have entered the King's Gate, and you are one of His pilgrims. Tonight you must sleep here, and tomorrow I will show you the way to the Heavenly City—the King's Way!"

CHAPTER 9

Christian Visits Interpreter

When the morning came, Christian felt rested, and ready for another day's journey. Goodwill brought him out and showed him a narrow pathway, which went straight across the open country.

"Are there any turnings?" asked Christian. "What shall I do if I come to a place where there are two roads?"

"The Way of the King is always quite straight," said Goodwill, "and all the paths that lead out of it are crooked. And the wrong paths are generally wide, while the right path is narrow. If you look carefully you will not mistake it."

"I wonder whether you could unfasten my burden for me?" asked Christian, when he was saying good-bye. "I could walk so much better without it."

"I cannot do that," said Goodwill. "You must carry it patiently until you come to the Cross, and then it will fall off, and you will never see it again."

"How glad I shall be!" sighed Christian. "Are there any other houses on the way besides this one?"

"Yes; about the middle of the day you will pass the house of Interpreter. He is very kind, and if you ask to see him he will show you many wonderful things in his house."

Young Christian's Pilgrimage

The morning was bright and pleasant, and Christian enjoyed his walk very much. The birds were singing so loudly that he felt as if he must sing with them, and the air was so fresh that it seemed to take away all the weariness which had troubled him in the City of Destruction.

"There is nothing to hurt me here," he thought. "Worldly did not speak the truth when he said I should be frightened."

Just when he was beginning to think that he would like to rest for a little while, he saw a large house standing near the road, and he knew that it must be the house of Interpreter. He went up to the door and knocked, and presently a servant came to ask what he wanted.

"I am a pilgrim," he said, "on my way to the King's City. I stayed at the Gate last night, and Goodwill told me that the master of this house is his friend. May I speak to him?"

The servant went back and called his master, and soon Interpreter came out. He was a tall man with a kind face and Christian thought he looked very wise.

He put his hand on the the boy's shoulder, saying, "What can I do for you?"

"Would you let me see some of the wonderful things in your house?" asked Christian. He spoke timidly, for he could not help thinking that, although Interpreter might be pleased to have grown-up visitors at his house, a young pilgrim like himself would perhaps be in the way. "Goodwill told me I could come to see you," he added.

Christian Visits Interpreter

Interpreter smiled. "Goodwill is my friend," he said. "Are you one of the King's pilgrims? Come in, and I will find some things that you will like to see." He took Christian's hand, and led him into the hall, where the servant was still waiting. Interpreter asked for a lamp, and when it was brought to him, he opened the door of a large room. Curtains were drawn across the windows, but the light of the lamp filled all the room with brightness. On the wall, opposite to the door, hung a picture, and when Christian saw it he stared and stood quite still.

It was the picture of a Man, whose face was more wonderful than anything which Christian had ever imagined. The Man was walking over a mountain path. All around Him, amongst the rocks, grew briars and thorns which had torn His garments in many places, and His feet were bleeding, for the rough stones had wounded them. In His arms He carried a lamb. It was tired, and had laid its head upon His shoulder, and the Man was looking down at it with gentle, loving eyes. Underneath the picture, in letters of gold, were written the words—

"HE WILL GATHER THE LAMBS TOGETHER AND CARRY THEM IN HIS ARMS."

"Was the lamb lost?" asked Christian.

"Yes," replied Interpreter; "lost and almost dead. Do you not see how tired it looks, and how its fleece is torn and soiled? But the Good Shepherd heard its cry, and He never rested until He had found it, and then he

35

brought it home in his arms."

"It must have been a hard path," said Christian; "the stones have cut the Man's feet."

"It was a very hard path, but He did not mind that, because He loved His lamb. I have shown you this picture first, because the Good Shepherd is our King's own Son, and just as a shepherd loves his flock, so He loves the pilgrims. The pilgrims are like the lambs. You can think of this when you are sad or frightened, and remember Who is watching over you."

"*I* am a pilgrim," said Christian suddenly, looking up at Interpreter.

"A pilgrim, and a lamb in the flock of the Good Shepherd. Now I will take you to see something else."

CHAPTER 10

Passion and Patience,
and the Brave Soldier

Christian was sorry to have to turn away from the
picture of the Good Shepherd. "I shall never forget it,"
he thought. "The Shepherd's face is so wonderful."

Interpreter now took Christian upstairs into a
children's playroom. Two small boys were sitting
there, each in his own chair. One of them appeared to
be quiet and happy, but the other was crying, and
seemed very cross and discontented.

"These two boys are staying here for a time," said
Interpreter. "The one who is crying is called Passion,
and his brother's name is Patience."

"Why is Passion crying?" asked Christian.

"He is a foolish boy," replied Interpreter. "There are
some beautiful gifts coming soon from the King, and
the children are each to have their share. Patience is
willing to wait for them, but Passion is upset because
he cannot enjoy them at once. He wishes to have his
pleasure *now,* instead of at the proper time!"

Just then the door opened, and a man came in
carrying a quantity of books and toys which he spread
upon the table before Passion. The boy was delighted,
and wiping away his tears, began to look at his
treasures. Among them were some bags filled with

bright, golden coins, and when Passion saw these he held them up in his hands and laughed at Patience, who had nothing with which to amuse himself.

"Passion is very happy now," said Interpreter, "but in a short time all his coins will be spent, and his presents will be torn and broken and spoiled, and when the *King's* gifts come he will have no share in them. Then he will wish he had waited as Patience is waiting."

"Are the King's gifts better than these?" asked Christian in surprise.

"Far better. They are treasures which cannot be spoiled, and Patience is very wise to wait for them."

"Passion is laughing now," said Christian, "but I think Patience will have the best of it in the end!"

"I am sure he will," replied Interpreter. "You must remember that everything I show you is meant to teach you something, and you may learn from this that it is not wise to wish too eagerly for pleasant things until the King sends them. He knows exactly what is good for each of us, and He will always give us what will make us really happy. If we behave like Passion and try to be happy in our own way, we are sure to be disappointed."

Interpreter now took Christian out of the house and through his garden, to a place from which they could see a beautiful palace, not very far off. The roof of the palace was flat, and upon it a number of people were walking about, dressed in garments which shone brightly like gold.

Passion and Patience, and the Brave Soldier

"Is that one of the King's palaces?" asked Christian.
"Yes; but it is not easy for anyone to enter it."
Outside the palace, Christian saw a great crowd of
men who looked as if they wanted to go in, but were
afraid to do so. Then he noticed that some other men,
in armour, were standing round the doorway. They had
fierce, cruel faces, and the men who were outside were
afraid to try to pass by them. A little way from the door
a man was sitting at a table, with a book before him, in
which he wrote the name of anyone who tried to get
into the palace.
Christian was very interested in all this, and he
hoped that one of the men would be brave enough to
go into the palace.
"Why does not the King drive away the wicked
soldiers?" he asked. "He *could* drive them away, and
then all those people could go into the palace."
"He could do it quite easily," replied Interpreter,
"but He wishes to see how many of the people really
care about entering the palace. Those who love the
King with all their hearts are not afraid of the soldiers.
We can wait for a little while, and you will see someone
go in."
So they sat down upon the grass, and Christian
watched the people. Presently a man came out from
the crowd and went towards the table near the
doorway. His name was written down in the book,
then he put on his helmet and drew his sword, and
rushed in among the soldiers. He fought with them for
a long time, and Christian thought he would be killed;

He got into the palace at last.

Passion and Patience, and the Brave Soldier

but although he received many wounds, he got into the palace at last, and then all the people upon the palace roof began to shout with joy.

Christian smiled. "Does that mean we are not to be frightened, because the King will help us, and take us safely into His City?"

"Yes," said Interpreter. "I thought you would understand it for yourself. Now, you have seen enough for one day. We must find a bed for you, and tomorrow you must continue on your journey."

CHAPTER 11

Christian Comes to the Cross

Christian slept very comfortably that night, and quite early in the morning he said good-bye to Interpreter and his family.

Beyond Interpreter's house the Way of the King was easy to find, for a high wall had been built on each side of the road. Christian thought this would make his journey easy, but Interpreter had told him that the wall did not go all the way to the Heavenly City.

"When you have passed it," he had said, "you must still keep to the straight path, and as long as you do that you will be safe."

Christian had almost forgotten his burden while he was with Interpreter, but as he walked along and the day began to grow hot, he felt its weight again and wished that he could get rid of it.

"Goodwill said I should lose it at the Cross," he thought. "I wonder if that is very far away?"

Presently he came to a place where there was a hill by the side of the road, and upon the hill he saw the very thing for which he was longing. There stood the Cross, and the moment Christian began to climb the path which led to it, he felt that the bands which fastened his burden were breaking. Then it fell from

Then it fell from his shoulders.

his shoulders, and rolled to the bottom of the hill, and when he turned to see what had become of it he found that it was gone out of sight.

At first he was so surprised that he could scarcely believe that he had really lost the burden which had been such a trouble to him.

"I must be dreaming," he thought; but although he stood still for a few minutes, and rubbed his eyes, the burden did not come back. The birds went on singing, and the sun shone brightly upon the Cross, and he knew that he must be awake, and that the King had really taken the weight from his shoulders for ever.

"Now I can walk as quickly as I like," he said to himself; but he stayed looking at the Cross, with his heart full of joy and thankfulness.

Christian remembered hearing about the King's own Son who had once come to visit the country in which he lived; but, although the King's Son was kind and good to everyone, many of the people hated Him. At last they seized Him, and put Him to death in a very cruel manner by nailing Him to a cross of wood. Pilgrims to the Heavenly City could look at the Cross and remember what had been done for them. Christian had read of all this in his Book, and as he stood near the Cross he thought how very good the King's Son must be, and he did not wonder any more why Evangelist and the other strangers never tired of talking about Him.

"Perhaps when they were pilgrims they carried burdens like mine," he said to himself. "Then, when they came to the Cross, they lost them, just as I have done. But I wish the people had not been so cruel to the King's Son!" And as he looked up at the Cross a tear came into his eyes.

Just then he heard a voice behind him saying, "Peace." Christian turned round quickly, and saw three angels standing close to him. They wore shining white robes, and when Christian looked at them his eyes felt dazzled, as if he had been gazing at the sun.

"They must have come from the Heavenly City," he thought; "they are so bright and beautiful!"

"You have often displeased the King," said one of the angels, "but I have come to tell you that He has quite forgiven you, and the wrong things which you have done will not be remembered any more."

Then the second took him by the hand, saying, "These clothes which you are wearing are torn and soiled. The King wishes His pilgrims to wear clothes which are clean, so He has given you some new ones."

And before Christian had time to think what answer he should make, his shabby clothes were taken away and he found himself dressed in new clothes of the King.

Then the third set the mark of the King upon his forehead, and gave him a roll of parchment, which was called the Roll of Faith; Christian was told he must be sure to take care of it, for he would be asked to show it at the gate of the Heavenly City.

After this the three angels went away, and Christian was left to think about all that the King had done for him. Christian knew that he belonged to the King for ever, now. He was one of the King's own children, and it made him very proud to think of it!

CHAPTER 12

Simple, Sloth, and Presumption

Christian now felt very happy as he walked along. "I have lost my burden," he said to himself, "and the King has given me these new clothes! I think I would have started this journey long ago if I had known how pleasant it is to be a pilgrim!"

Then he remembered his friend Christiana, and he thought what a pity it was that she had not come with him. But he did not know how she would have managed it, for she had three brothers, besides her baby sister, and she had to take care of them all.

"Perhaps when I get to the City I can ask the King to send someone to help her, for I should like her to come too."

Then he wondered whether his mother had told the King that she had left him in the City of Destruction, and whether she would know that his burden had now been taken away.

Christian looked down once more at the clothes which the angels had given him. "They are so clean, and they are not the least bit hot and heavy, as my old ones were."

He was walking on with his mind full of these things when he saw, just before him, three boys lying upon the grass by the side of the road. He stopped to look at them and saw that they were all fast asleep, and that their feet were bound together with bands of iron.

The day was very hot, and these boys had foolishly left the path and lain down to rest for a little while. The servants of the Wicked Prince were always on the watch for careless pilgrims, and as soon as the lads were asleep they had hurried to bind their feet, so that, unless the King Himself sent someone to help them, they would never be able to take another step towards the Heavenly City.

Christian felt that it would be unkind to leave them lying there, so he went up to them and woke them.

"You had better get up," he said. "This is not at all a safe place to sleep in. Don't you know that someone has bound your feet together?"

Then one of them, whose name was Simple, answered, without even opening his eyes, "What is the matter? I don't see anything to hurt. Let us have a minute's peace!"

But Christian said, "I am sure you are in great danger. Make haste, and let me help you to undo these irons!"

The boy who lay next to Simple was named Sloth, and at last he sat up and, in keeping with his name, began to rub his eyes in a very sleepy way. He looked at Christian, but he would not listen to his advice.

"What is the use of disturbing us?" he said. "Just go on. I shall be coming soon. when I have had a good rest!"

Simple, Sloth, and Presumption

And the third boy, who was called Presumption, said, "Surely we can do as we like! If we choose to sleep in a dangerous place it is our business, not yours; so go on your journey, and don't meddle with other people!"

Then they both lay down again by the side of Simple, and in a few minutes Christian saw that they were all sleeping as soundly as before. It was of no use for him to waste his time over such idle, foolish boys, so he was obliged to turn away, feeling very sorry that they would not listen to him, or believe that they were in the power of the Wicked Prince.

He saw two boys climbing upon the wall.

CHAPTER 13

Formalist and Hypocrisy

When Christian had gone some distance from the place where the three boys lay sleeping, he turned and looked back, thinking that perhaps they might now be fully awake, and more anxious to be freed from their iron fetters. But he could not see anything of them, and he was just moving on again when he heard a noise on his left hand, and saw two boys climbing upon the wall. They both dropped over into the Way of the King, and seeing Christian they ran up to him.

"Where have you come from?" he asked.

The boys, whose names were Formalist and Hypocrisy, answered, "We have been living in the land of Vainglory, but we are now starting our journey to the Heavenly City to see the King."

"But don't you know," said Christian, "that you should have come in at the Gate?"

"Oh," cried the boys, "that Gate is much too far from our country! We just made a short cut across the fields, and came over the wall."

Christian was certain that the King would not like people to begin their pilgrimage in this way, so he said, "I am afraid you ought not to have done this."

"Oh, don't you bother about it," they said. "Our

people never go round by that Gate. Besides, what does it matter, so long as we get on to the right road? You came in by the Gate, and we came over the wall, and now we are all in exactly the same place."

"I still don't think you ought to have done it," said Christian.

"What nonsense!" they replied. "We are just as good pilgrims as you are, except that you have such fine clothes, which very likely somebody had to give you because your own were not fit to be seen!"

This was a very unkind speech, and Christian felt inclined to answer back in the same way. But he had read in his Book that the King's servants ought always to speak gently, even when angry words were spoken to them, so he waited a minute and then said quietly, "That is quite true. My clothes *were* all spoilt and shabby, and the King gave me these clothes Himself. It was very kind of Him, and I am very glad He did it, because now I am sure that when I get to the City, He will know that I am one of His own pilgrims. And the angel has set the mark of the King on my forehead, and I have a Roll of Faith which I am to show at the end of my journey. You have not any of these things, because you did not come in at the Gate!"

But the boys only laughed, so Christian walked on ahead by himself.

Presently they all came to the foot of a hill called Difficulty. There was one path over the hill and two others which ran around each side. The Way of the King led over the hill. It was very rough and very steep,

Formalist and Hypocrisy

but Christian knew that he must not turn away from it. A spring of cool water was flowing just by the wayside, so, as he was very thirsty, he had a refreshing drink and then began to climb the rocky path.

Formalist and Hypocrisy also saw the two paths, which turned one to the right and the other to the left out of the straight road.

"What is the good of climbing up that steep place?" they said. "These two paths are smooth and easy, and as they go round the hill they must join up with the King's Way again on the other side."

So Formalist said, "I will go along this path," and Hypocrisy said, "I will go along that one." The boys parted, believing that they would meet again very soon.

Now, if they had entered by the Gate they would have known, as Christian did, that the straight road was the only safe one; but both these boys were as good as lost, because they had not taken the trouble to obey the King and begin their pilgrimage in the right way.

Formalist and Hypocrisy, whose names meant "show" and "pretence," found it too hard to pretend they were following the King's Way any longer.

Formalist had entered the path of Danger, and very soon he found himself in a great wood. He wandered about for many nights and days, but he could not find his way out of it, and so at last he collapsed with hunger and cold.

The path of Destruction, which Hypocrisy had chosen, was no better. It led into the midst of some dark mountains, where the boy went up and down until his foot slipped and he fell, wounding himself upon the sharp rocks, so that he too lay there without help.

CHAPTER 14

The Hill Difficulty

Christian found the path up the hillside a very hard one. It was covered with rough stones and sharp pieces of rock which hurt his feet, and it became steeper and steeper as he went on, until at last he was obliged to climb upon his hands and knees. The sun was now shining very brightly, for it was the middle of the day, and its rays fell upon Christian and made him feel hot and tired.

"What *should* I have done if I had had to climb this hill yesterday?" he thought. "I could never have carried my burden up such a dreadful road!"

When he was about halfway up the hill the path became easier. He was able to walk again, and the stones did not seem to be quite so sharp. Still, it was hard work climbing, and when he came presently to a shady shelter he was very glad indeed. This shelter had been built by order of the King, so that His pilgrims might have a place in which to rest on their way over the hill.

Christian went in and sat down. It was cool and quiet, and he thought he would now have time to look at the Roll of Faith which the angel had given to him; so he took it out and read it for a little while. Then,

Their faces were white with fear.

The Hill Difficulty

instead of making haste to the top of the hill, he sat in the shelter, looking at his new clothes and thinking of many things, until his eyes closed and he fell asleep.

He did not wake until quite late in the afternoon, and when he looked at the sky and saw that it was already beginning to grow crimson with the sunset, he jumped up and began to walk as quickly as he could.

Before he reached the top of the hill he met two boys running down very fast indeed. Their faces were white with fear, and their whole bodies were trembling, but when they saw Christian they stopped to speak to him.

"What is the matter?" he asked. "You are running the wrong way."

"Oh," cried the eldest, whose name was Timorous, "we were going to the City of the King, and we had climbed up this terrible hill, but the farther we go the more danger we find, so we are hurrying home again!"

"Yes," said the other, who was called Mistrust, "there are two great lions lying in the path, and we don't know whether they are asleep or not; but I am sure if we try to pass them we shall be torn to pieces!"

Then Christian began to feel frightened too, and he said, "What shall I do?"

"Why, come back with us!" said Timorous. "You cannot be so foolish as to venture near those savage beasts!"

"I don't know," replied Christian. "If I go back I shall never see the King."

"Well, you certainly will not see Him if you go on," said Mistrust, "for the lions will kill you!"

Young Christian's Pilgrimage

But Christian remembered that Evangelist and Goodwill and Interpreter had all told him that, although he might often be frightened and in trouble, the King would help him and take care of him.

"I don't think I will turn back," he said. "The lions may not be awake. Let us all go together."

"Oh, no!" cried Timorous and Mistrust; "we dare not. We shall just make our way home again, and be very thankful when we get there safely."

So they ran down the hill, and left Christian to go on his way alone.

He could not help being frightened, and he thought, "I will look at my Roll of Faith, and see whether there is anything written in it about these lions."

But when he put his hand into his pocket the Roll was not there, and though he felt carefully amongst his clothes, he could not find it anywhere.

"Where *can* it be?" he said, and he stood still to think how he could possibly have lost it. He was in great trouble, for he remembered that the angel had told him to take care of the Roll, for he would be asked to show it at the gate of the Heavenly City.

"I cannot go without it," he cried. "Oh, what shall I do?" And he began to feel very afraid.

CHAPTER 15

Christian Comes to the Palace Beautiful

The loss of the Roll of Faith made poor Christian very worried. He soon forgot all about the lions in his trouble, and could think only of his carelessness in losing the most precious of the King's gifts. Suddenly he remembered the shady shelter in which he had spent the afternoon. Perhaps the Roll had fallen there, and when he had jumped up so hurriedly he might not have seen it.

"Oh, how could I be so foolish!" he cried. "I ought only to have rested there a little while, and I wasted so much time, and now it will be night before I reach the top of the hill!"

He turned round and went back slowly, looking carefully at the path lest he might have dropped the Roll of Faith on his way. At last he reached the shelter, and there on the floor, just under the bench where he had been sitting, he saw his lost treasure.

Eagerly he caught it up, and how thankful he felt to the King for letting him find it again!

But this search for the Roll had delayed Christian, and although he climbed the steep path once more as quickly as he could, the sun had gone out of sight before he reached the top of the hill, and the light was fading

There was only a small space between the lions.

Christian Comes to the Palace Beautiful

very fast.

"It is all my own fault," he thought. "If I had not been so lazy I should not have lost my Roll of Faith, and I might have had time to find a place to rest before night."

Then he remembered the lions, and wondered how far he was from the spot where they lay. He knew that these savage beasts would prowl about in search of their prey during the darkness, and as the shadows grew deeper and deeper round him he felt more and more afraid.

Just when the light had become very dim indeed a large building appeared in the distance, and as Christian hurried along he saw that it was a great palace, and that the Way of the King would lead him close to its gates. A cottage stood just inside the gates. He supposed this must be the caretaker's lodge, and he walked quickly towards it, hoping he might be allowed to stay there for the night.

The path now became very narrow indeed, and when he had almost reached the palace gates, Christian saw the two lions which had so frightened Mistrust and Timorous. They were lying just before him, one on each side of the path. The lions were chained, but it was too dark for the chains to be seen, and Christian stood still, wondering what he should do. There was only a small space between the lions, and he thought that if he attempted to pass them they would surely spring upon him.

The name of the gatekeeper was Watchful, and he knew how much the pilgrims feared the lions, so he

Young Christian's Pilgrimage

came very often to the door of his house to see if anyone was coming near. When he saw Christian he called to him, saying, "Don't be frightened; the lions are both chained. Keep in the middle of the path, and they will not hurt you."

So Christian went on, trembling and very much afraid, but he was careful to keep in the middle of the path. So although the great creatures roared as he walked between them, they did not even stretch out their huge paws to touch him.

When he had passed the lions Christian shouted out loud for joy, and ran quickly towards Watchful, who stood at the gates.

"What palace is this?" Christian asked.

"It is called the Palace Beautiful," said Watchful, "and it belongs to the King. He built it for his pilgrims to use. Are you going to the Heavenly City?"

"Yes," answered Christian. "I slept last night at the house of Interpreter. May I stay here until the morning?"

"How is it that you are travelling so late?" asked Watchful.

Then Christian told of his long sleep in the afternoon, and how he had lost his Roll of Faith, and had gone back to look for it.

"Well," said Watchful, "I will call the lady of the house, and as you are one of the King's pilgrims she will take care of you."

So they went together to the door of the palace and Watchful rang the bell.

CHAPTER 16

New Friends

Christian waited by the side of Watchful in the porch of the Palace Beautiful, and presently a lady came out to speak to them. Her name was Discretion, and Christian knew that from her name she would be very careful and thoughtful in everything she did.

"Why did you call me?" Discretion asked; and then seeing Christian, she put out her hand and laid it on his shoulder.

"She is rather like my mother," Christian thought. "I will listen carefully to all she tells me."

Watchful answered Discretion, saying, "This boy is journeying to the Heavenly City, and it is too late for him to walk any farther tonight, so he would be glad to stay here if you are willing to take him in."

Then Discretion asked Christian many questions. She wished to know from what city he had come, and why he had left his home. She also asked him who had directed him into the Way of the King. Christian told her all that had happened to him on his journey.

"And what is your name?" she asked at last.

"Christian," he replied. "I would be so glad if you let me stay here until the morning."

"Yes, you may stay," answered Discretion, smiling

at Christian's anxious face. "Wait, and I will cal' my daughters."

She went back into the house and brought out three girls. Two of them were older than Christian. Their names were Piety and Prudence. Charity, the youngest, was just about his own age. "This is one of the King's pilgrims," said their mother. "I think we can make room for him in the palace, can we not?"

"Oh, yes!" said Prudence; and Charity ran up to him and held onto his arm, as Christiana had sometimes done before he left the city.

"Come in," said Piety. "We are very glad to see you."

A number of people were in the hall of the palace, and they all looked kindly at Christian as he came in.

"Mother takes care of the pilgrims," said Charity. "We girls help her look after them."

"It is not quite time for supper," said Discretion to her daughters, "but no doubt Christian is tired. Take him into your own room, and let him rest."

The three girls led the way to a large room, where a lamp was burning and casting its cheerful light upon walls which were covered with pictures. Here Christian sat down, while Piety and Prudence took up the needlework which they had laid aside when their mother called for them. Charity brought a footstool, and seated herself near to Christian. She was a kind-hearted girl, and loved to spend her time in helping her mother's guests, and in doing all she could to make them happy; for her name, Charity, meant "caring love."

"If you are not too tired to talk," said Piety, "we

New Friends

should like to hear about your journey. What made you leave your home?"

"I was frightened," answered Christian; "for the strangers who came to our city used to tell us that it would be destroyed."

"And how was it that you thought of coming into the Way of the King?"

"I had read of the Heavenly City in my Book, and one day Evangelist met me, and he showed me the way to the Gate to the King's Way."

"Did you stay at the house of Interpreter?"

"Oh, yes," replied Christian. "He was very kind to me. I saw the picture of the Good Shepherd, and I watched a soldier fight his way into the palace. I wish I could have stayed there a long time!"

"And what have you done today?"

"First, I passed by the Cross, and there I lost my burden, and the angels brought me these new clothes. They gave me a message from the King, and one of them set this mark upon my forehead. After that I found three boys sleeping by the wayside. I tried to wake them, but they would not listen to me. Then young Formalist and Hypocrisy climbed over the wall, but I think they chose the wrong path when we came to the hill, for I did not see them again."

"The hill is hard to climb," said Piety.

"Yes, I thought I should never get up; and then, when I saw the lions, I very nearly turned back again, but Watchful called to me, and told me they were chained."

"Do you ever think about your old home?" asked Prudence.

"Yes," said Christian; "I often think about it."

"Have you sometimes wished to go back again?"

"Once or twice, when I have been very tired; but I am sure the Heavenly City is far better than ours, and I know I will be happy when I get there."

"Why will you be happy?"

"I will see the Prince," said Christian. "It was cruel of those people to nail him to the Cross, and I love Him because He died for our sakes. My mother is with the King. She went away when I was young."

"Have you any brothers or sisters?" asked Charity.

"No, but my friend Christiana used to play with me, and she has brothers, and a sister."

"Why didn't you bring her with you?" asked Charity. "Then you would have had someone to talk to on the way."

"She did not believe what the strangers said," replied Christian; "and she has her three brothers and her sister to take care of. They have no father or mother, and Christiana has to do everything herself."

"Didn't you talk to her, and beg her to come with you?"

"I often told her about the City, but, you know, I might not have come myself if Evangelist had not shown me the way. Then I started at once, so that I didn't even say good-bye to Christiana."

"Well, perhaps Evangelist will find her, and then she will come and bring her brothers and sister with her."

New Friends

Just at this moment a bell rang, and the two elder girls folded up their work, saying, "That is to tell us that our supper is ready."

Christian was hungry as well as tired, and he enjoyed the good food which was set before him. After supper the girls' mother, Discretion, took him upstairs into a pleasant room with a window looking towards the east, and there the weary pilgrim slept soundly until he was awakened by the light of the rising sun.

CHAPTER 17

A Happy Day

When morning came Christian supposed he would have to continue his journey, but as soon as breakfast was over he heard Discretion calling him.

"I think it will do you good to stay with us for a few days," she said. "You have walked a long way since you left home, and it is not well for young pilgrims to travel too quickly at first."

"I should like to stay," said Christian, "if I am not in the way."

"You will not be in the way at all. Taking care of pilgrims is part of the work which my daughters have to do for the King, and we are always glad to have children staying at the palace."

"Did my mother stay here? Her name was Peace, and I think she must have come this way when the King sent for her. It was a long time ago."

"We will look in the records for her name. If she stayed here it will be written down."

"I think she was a little, just a *little* bit like you," said Christian quietly.

Discretion bent down. "You *will* find her again, Christian," she said quietly.

"I shall see her in the King's City."

"Yes, and then you will never lose her again."

"And my father?" asked Christian, anxiously. "Will he *always* be busy, or do you think he will some day be able to come too?"

"I cannot tell," replied Discretion, showing her careful and thoughtful nature. "I am sure the King will not leave off sending messages to him, and perhaps when he knows that you and your mother are so happy he will wish to be with you, and he will begin his pilgrimage."

"He will not be frightened on the way," said Christian, "because he is very brave. I think, perhaps, even mother did not like passing the lions. When my father comes, will you tell him that I stayed here, and that when he gets to the gates of the Heavenly City he will be sure to see me watching for him?"

"Yes, I will tell him," answered Discretion. "Now I have many things to do, so Charity will take you into the library, and you may look in the records for your mother's name."

Christian spent a very happy day at the palace. Sometimes Charity was with him, and sometimes Prudence, and sometimes Piety, but they were all kind, and did everything they could to please their guest.

Christian, like many other boys, loved to read stories, and he found much to enjoy in the library of the Palace Beautiful. There were many stories of children: Moses; Samuel lighting the lamps in the House of God; and young Timothy listening to his mother's teaching.

A Happy Day

"And this is our Prince Himself," said Piety. "You have read in your Book how He came down to live amongst us, and was a Baby in a poor home. Here you see Him in the arms of His mother, and the shepherds are kneeling round Him."

Christian liked this picture, and stood before it for some time, until Charity called him to look at one which was her favourite. It was called "The Guardian Angel." A child was walking along a very narrow path, and close behind him came an angel, with hands spread out to touch the child's shoulders on either side.

"You see, he cannot fall," said Charity. "The King has sent the angel, and if the child slips, the angel will hold fast."

The time passed so quickly that Christian was quite surprised when the evening came. Discretion had been busy all day, but before the lamps were lighted she came into the library where Christian was reading. He laid down his book, and she sat with him and talked to him, telling him many things about their good King and the Prince, His Son.

"I have never spent such a happy day in all my life," said Christian, when he went to bed. "If it were not that I wish so much to live in the King's City, I should like to stay here always!"

CHAPTER 18

Christian Receives His Armour

Christian spent three whole days at the Palace Beautiful. On the second day Discretion allowed him to see the armoury. This was a large room, in which were stored all kinds of weapons for the use of the King's servants.

Here Christian saw long rows of shining helmets, shields, breastplates of the finest brass, glittering swords, and shoes which Charity told him could never be worn out. Christian noticed that these things were not all intended for grown-up persons. There were helmets which he felt sure were too small even for him, and swords which seemed only fit for young children to play with.

"Are they toys?" he asked.

"No," said Piety; "they are for the youngest pilgrims."

Then Christian could not help thinking how very much he would like to have a sword and shield of his own, and be one of the King's soldiers.

Piety sat down by the window in the armoury, and told Christian about the wonderful things which some of the King's soldiers had done. The story he liked best was that of a boy named David, who had fought with a great giant, and had been able to kill him.

Young Christian's Pilgrimage

"The giant was one of the King's enemies," said Piety, "and he thought he could easily kill David. He was covered with armour from head to foot, and David wore only a shepherd's clothes, and carried neither sword nor spear.

"What did he fight with?" asked Christian.

"He had a sling and a stone, and when he threw the stone at the giant the King helped him, and he aimed so well that he struck the giant on the forehead and killed him."

This story comforted Christian, for if the King had helped David, no doubt He would be ready to help any other young pilgrim who trusted in Him.

On the third day Christian said to Prudence, "Is it time for me to go on with my journey?"

"Not yet," answered Prudence. "It is misty this morning, and you have not seen the view from the roof of the palace. You must wait for the mist to clear."

So Christian spent another happy and peaceful day.

The next morning, when he opened his window, he found that the mist had all passed away, and as soon as breakfast was over the three girls took him up to the roof. It was flat, so that people could walk upon it, or even sit there in the pleasant summer weather.

Christian looked towards the south, and far away in the distance he could see a long range of beautiful hills, with broad green fields, and vineyards, and shady woods. He could even see the streams sparkling in the sunlight, as they flowed down into the quiet valleys.

"Oh," he exclaimed, "what a lovely country that

must be!"

"Yes," said Piety. "That is Emmanuel's Land, and the Way of the King passes through it. The hills are called the Delectable Mountains, and from them you will be able to see the gates of the Heavenly City."

"Will it take me long to get there?" asked Christian.

"I do not know," answered Piety; "you are a young pilgrim, and you cannot travel very fast."

Just then they heard the voice of Discretion calling to them.

"We must let Christian start in good time," she said, "in order to reach the valley before the sun is hot."

"I am quite ready," began Christian, but young Charity interrupted him.

"No, he is not ready—is he, mother? We have something more to do for him, have we not?"

"Yes," replied Discretion, and she led the way to the armoury. "Between the palace and the Heavenly City the King's enemies are often very troublesome, and even young pilgrims need to carry weapons."

Christian glowed with pleasure when he found that he was really to have a suit of armour for his very own, and Discretion and her daughters seemed pleased also.

"I like to see you made into a soldier," said Charity; and Christian wished that Christiana could have been there too.

"You must take care of your armour," said Discretion, as she chose out a helmet of the right size. "It must always be kept bright and shining."

Then Piety brought him a shield, which was just

large enough to protect him, and not too heavy for him to carry.

Prudence fastened the sword at his side, and Charity fitted on his shoes. Then, when he was completely dressed, Discretion bent down and said quietly, "May the blessing of the King go with you, my child, and may you continue His faithful soldier and servant all the days of your life!"

Christian felt too happy to speak, so he just held tightly onto Discretion, as if she had been his own mother, and she understood quite well that his heart was full of love and gratitude. "You must thank the King," she said. "It is He Who gives you all these things!"

CHAPTER 19

An Enemy

Watchful was standing at the door of the lodge when Christian came out of the palace. When he was opening the gates he told Christian that another young pilgrim had passed by.

"I asked him his name," said the gatekeeper, "and he told me it was Faithful."

"Oh," cried Christian, "I know him very well! His house was quite near to ours in the City of Destruction. How long has he been gone? Do you think I can catch up with him?"

"It is about half an hour since I saw him," replied Watchful. "I should think by this time he will be at the bottom of the hill."

Christian was so pleased at the thought of having a companion that he determined to walk as quickly as possible, in order to meet with Faithful. But first he must say good-bye to his friends, who had all come down to the gates with him.

"It is a beautiful morning," said Discretion. "Suppose we walk to the foot of the hill with Christian?"

"That would be very nice," said Charity, "and perhaps we may find Faithful there. I wonder why he did not come in to see us?"

Young Christian's Pilgrimage

"It is early," said Discretion, "and no doubt he wished to hasten on his journey."

The Palace Beautiful was built at the top of Hill Difficulty. There was a valley below, and the path which led down into it from the gates of the palace was very steep indeed.

"It is difficult to get up this hill, and dangerous to go down," Christian observed.

"Yes," replied Prudence, "people sometimes have bad falls upon this path."

It was not long before they found themselves in the valley, and then Discretion gave Christian a bag of food which she had brought with her.

"We have been very glad to see you," she said, "and I shall not forget to give your message to your father when he comes to the palace."

Christian was quite sorry to say good-bye, and when Discretion and her daughters had left him he felt very lonely indeed. The valley was quiet and cool, and he walked on quickly, hoping soon to see Faithful in the distance before him; but, instead of Faithful, he presently saw a very evil-looking man coming along the path to meet him. The man was tall and strong, and his face was not a pleasant one. As he drew near, Christian thought he might even be the Wicked Prince himself!

"He is the King's enemy," thought Christian, "and he will try to hurt me. What shall I do?"

At first he thought he would turn round and run back towards the foot of the hill. Discretion might look

An Enemy

back and see him, or perhaps Watchful might be at the palace gates and would send someone to help him. Then he remembered that he had no armour for his back, and that his breastplate and shield would be of no use to him unless he *faced* his enemy. So he determined to trust in the King and go straight on. Perhaps, as he was only a boy, the enemy would pass by without taking any notice of him. He walked on steadily, and in a few minutes the man was quite close.

"My name is Apollyon. I should like to know where *you* have come from!" he said loudly, stopping in front of Christian, and looking down at his bright armour.

Christian felt very much frightened, but he answered, "From the City of Destruction."

"And where are you going?"

"To the City of the King."

"Perhaps you have forgotten," said Apollyon, "that the City of Destruction belongs to me. If you were not a boy, who can be taken back again, I should kill you for running away without my leave!"

"I know the city belongs to you," replied Christian bravely, "but the King loves me better than you do, and I would rather live with Him!"

Apollyon smiled. "Don't be foolish!" he said. "I can be very kind to people when I like them, and if you will come back with me, and promise not to run away again, I will not be angry with you. You shall live in my house, and be one of my own servants!"

"I am one of the *King's* servants," said Christian.

"That does not matter. The King's servants often

run away from Him. Besides, you were *my* servant when you were at home, and you ought to be very glad that I am willing to forgive you, and take you back again!"

Poor Christian felt himself beginning to tremble, but he answered, "I love the King, and I would rather be *His* servant. Now, let me go on!"

But the King's enemy had made up his mind that Christian should go home with him, so he said, "Don't be in a hurry! Just think of all the trouble you will meet with on the way. My soldiers are up and down everywhere, and if they see you and try to hurt you, I don't suppose the King will take the trouble to help you. You know you have served Him very badly since you set out. You were so careless that you fell into the Slough of Despair. You let Worldly deceive you and turn you out of the right path. Then you slept in the shelter, and nearly lost your Roll of Faith. When you came in sight of the lions you were very nearly turning back for fear of them. And yet, at the Palace Beautiful, you talked as if you were one of the King's most *faithful* servants! I don't know how you can expect Him to do anything for *you!*"

Christian knew that all these things were true, and he wondered how Apollyon had heard about them.

"I have been very sorry," he said, "and the King has forgiven me. He knows I am a young pilgrim."

Then Apollyon could not keep back his anger any longer. He had been speaking gently, because he wished Christian to leave the King by choice, but when

An Enemy

he saw that his words were of no use he became fierce with rage.

"I hate your King," he cried, "and everybody and everything belonging to Him! You are *my* servant, and you shall never go to the Heavenly City, for I will destroy you!"

CHAPTER 20

The First Battle

Christian had scarcely time to put up his shield before Apollyon began to throw fiery darts at him, and he feared that he would soon be badly injured by them. But he remembered the story he had heard at the Palace Beautiful of David and the giant, and he thought, "David had only his shepherd's clothes, and I am wearing the good armour which the King has given me. I will trust in Him, and try not to be afraid, for I belong to the King now."

So he held his shield firmly on his arm, and caught nearly all Apollyon's darts upon it, until the evil enemy became wild with fury, and rushing suddenly at Christian he seized him in his strong arms. Those darts which Christian had not been able to catch upon his shield had struck him, and wounded him in his hands and feet. His wounds were very sore, and were bleeding so much that he was beginning to feel faint.

Apollyon had seen this, and he flung the boy upon the ground, thinking he would now be able to kill him. Christian drew out his sword from its sheath, but when Apollyon threw him down, it fell from his hand, and as he lay on the path he thought he had now no chance of escaping from his cruel enemy. Then, just as Apollyon was going to strike his last blow, Christian called to the King, and saw that the sword lay within his reach. He put out his hand and caught it up, and before Apollyon had time to prevent him, he thrust it into his attacker's body, and gave him a terrible wound!

The Wicked Prince could not bear the pain of a wound given with one of the King's swords, and he cried out loudly when Christian struck him. Then the boy's courage came back to him, and he thrust the weapon at his enemy a second time. With that, Apollyon fled away across the valley, and Christian was left alone.

He lay for a minute upon the path, and then he got up and looked round. All over the grass lay the sharp darts which had been thrown at him, but the King's enemy was gone. Christian could not see him anywhere.

"It was the King Who helped me," he thought, and his heart was full of thankfulness for his wonderful deliverance.

But Christian had been quite badly wounded, and he felt so weak and that he was obliged to sit down upon the grass and lean his head against a great rock. After a few minutes he fell asleep, and as he slept restlessly he dreamt that his wounds were being healed by the King's Son.

When Christian awoke at last, his arms and legs had stopped bleeding and did not even ache. Then he remembered that Discretion had given him some food, so he sat still for a little while and ate the bread and meat which was in the bag.

The First Battle

"I must make haste," he thought, "for I have lost so much time. I wonder whether Apollyon has really gone away, or whether he will come back to look for me again? And he said his soldiers were always around. I must be ready to meet them!"

So keeping his sword in his hand, and looking carefully from side to side among the rocks and bushes, young Christian continued along the King's Way.

CHAPTER 21

The Dark Valley

It was late in the afternoon when Christian came to the end of that valley. He had seen nothing more of his enemy, and he was beginning to think that he might now put his sword back into its sheath, when he saw two boys running towards him. Their faces were white, as those of Mistrust and Timorous had been, and as they came up to him, Christian said to them, "Where are you going?"

"Back! back!" cried the boys. "And if you care for your life you had better come with us!"

"Why?" asked Christian. "What is the matter?"

"Matter?" they answered. "We were going to the Heavenly City, but we have been as far as we dare. Indeed, if we had ventured a few steps farther, we should never have had the chance to come back and warn you!"

"What did you find?" said Christian, wondering what dangers he might have to pass through that night. He had no intention of turning back, for his victory over Apollyon had made him love and trust his good King more than ever; but he wished to know what the boys had seen, so that he might be prepared to defend himself.

"Just before us," they said, "is the Dark Valley; but we saw it in time, and we have hurried away."

"What is it like?"

"It is terrible! It is the most dreadful place we have ever seen, full of darkness, and we could hear cries and groans. No doubt they are made by pilgrims who have been lost there."

"But the Way of the King leads straight through it," said Christian.

"Yes," replied the boys.

"Then I do not see how we are to avoid it."

"*You* can try it if you like," they said; "but if *we* are to get the City at all, it must be by some other road than that!"

So they left him, and Christian went on, keeping his sword ready in his hand.

The Dark Valley lay much lower than the last valley. It was narrow, and the black rocks seemed almost to meet high above Christian's head as he entered it. The evening was coming on, and the path was soon surrounded with a thick mist, so that he could scarcely see his hand when he stretched it out before him. Flashes of light kept breaking through the mist, but he did not know whether they were flames of fire or of lightning, and the air was filled with terrible sounds which made his heart beat fast with fear. By the flashes of light he saw that the path upon which he was walking was indeed a very dangerous one. On his right hand there was a very deep pit, and on his left a marsh, and it was all he could do to prevent himself from

Christian enters the Dark Valley.

slipping into either one or the other.

Christian knew that this walk through the Dark Valley was going to be the worst part of his pilgrimage so far. Although he tried to think of the King and His kindness, he could not help being frightened. In one part of the valley some of the Wicked Prince's servants were waiting to trouble the pilgrims. A man came up behind him and whispered unpleasant words in his ear. Christian could not see the man, and he was so confused that he imagined that he had said these words himself, and he was afraid then that the King would be sad.

About the middle of the night, as Christian was walking carefully along in the darkness, he heard footsteps in the distance. Some people were coming towards him, shouting and uttering dreadful cries. He knew that this must be a band of the Wicked Prince's servants, and he thought, "They will attack me, and perhaps even kill me."

Christian wondered whether he should turn back, for he was becoming so frightened that his whole body was trembling. But he had already come a long distance through the valley, and he said to himself, "Perhaps I am not far from the end of it, and going back might be worse than going forward."

Presently he found that the soldiers had taken a different path, and he did not meet them at all.

Christian was comforted now in his loneliness by hearing the voice of a young pilgrim who was repeating aloud some of the words which were written

The Dark Valley

in the King's Book. It was too dark for him to see that
the pilgrim was Faithful, but he hoped that it might be
him, and that they would soon be able to meet with
each other. At last Christian called out, but although
Faithful heard Christian speak, he did not know who
might be wishing to stop him, so he made no answer.
Still, Christian knew another pilgrim was there, and
felt less frightened than when he had thought himself
to be alone.

CHAPTER 22

Christian Meets With Faithful

Christian had no rest that night. He did not dare to lie down and sleep in the Dark Valley, for he feared that the soldiers, whom he could hear passing up and down amongst the rocks, should find him, and put him to death, or carry him back to the City of Destruction. He was very tired, but he walked bravely on through the mist and darkness, praying in his heart that the King would watch over him. After a time he thought of some words which he had read in the King's Book. "God will put his angels in charge of you."

Then he remembered the picture which Charity loved so much, of the child with the Guardian Angel.

"The picture was true," he said to himself. "That child was walking on a path like this, and the King's angel was there to keep guard. Perhaps there is an angel with me now!"

At last the mist began to roll away, and a soft pale light shone overhead. Christian looked up, and found that he could now see a strip of sky between the overhanging rocks, and he knew that the day was breaking. As the sun rose and its strong, bright rays streamed even into the Dark Valley, Christian stood still and looked behind. The black rocks which surrounded him, and the narrow track with the treacherous marsh on one side and the steep precipice on the other, seemed even more dangerous than they had done in the darkness. Christian wondered how he had ever come safely through such a dreadful place!

Then he looked forward, and felt more and more thankful that the sun had risen, for he saw that the rest of the path was strewn with snares and nets, which evil soldiers had laid there to hinder and hurt the King's pilgrims. They had also dug holes in dangerous places, and had done everything they could to make the road difficult and unsafe, so that Christian thought, "If I had passed over it in the darkness I should very likely have fallen and injured myself!"

At the end of the Dark Valley there was a large cave in the side of the mountain, and in this cave two very powerful giants had once lived. Whenever pilgrims passed by their dwelling the giants attacked them, and for a long time this was one of the most dangerous places on the way to the Heavenly City. But one of the giants died, and the other grew old, and his limbs became stiff, so that he had no strength left, and Christian passed on safely.

The Dark Valley, with all its terrors, now lay behind Christian. Just before him the ground rose a little. He climbed quickly up the path, and when he reached the top of the hill he found that he could see for some distance along the road.

Not very far from him a boy was walking with his face towards the King's City. He was wearing new clothes, like Christian's own, but he had no armour over them.

"It must be Faithful," thought Christian, and he called out, "Wait for me, and I will walk with you!" Then Faithful looked round and Christian called again, "Wait till I can talk with you!"

But Faithful answered, "I am going to the King, and there are enemies behind me."

When Christian saw that Faithful would not wait for him, he began to run as fast as he could. He soon caught up with Faithful, and instead of stopping by his side he ran on further, so that Faithful in his turn was left behind. Christian laughed now, to think that he was ahead. But he forgot to look where he was going, and striking his foot against a stone, he fell to the ground and Faithful had to hurry and help him to get up.

CHAPTER 23

Faithful Tells the Story of His Pilgrimage

The two boys were very pleased to see each other, for they had been friends when they were living in the City of Destruction. Faithful had always been quiet and thoughtful, and he and Christian had sometimes talked together about the King's Book, and the wonderful stories which the strangers had told them.

"I am glad I have met with you," said Christian. "It will be much better for us to travel together."

"I wanted to come all the way with you," replied Faithful, "but you left the City of Destruction so suddenly that I did not know you were going to make the journey until you were gone."

"How long did you stay in the City?"

"Only two or three more days. After you left, the others talked a great deal about the King's messages, but I don't think they really believed them."

"What did they say to Pliable?"

"Oh, they soon found out where he had been, for he was covered all over with mud when he came back. They laughed at him, and would not let him talk with them."

"They need not have laughed at him," said Christian: "*they* did not start out!"

Young Christian's Pilgrimage

"No, but they made fun of him for turning back at the first bit of trouble he came to. I met him the day after, and I was going to ask him about you, but he crossed over the street and pretended he didn't see me."

"I am very sorry," said Christian. "I thought he would be a real pilgrim, and it was a pity that he went home again. Now, tell me all that has happened to you."

"I did not fall into the Slough," said Faithful; "but I met a girl named Pleasure before I came to the Gate. She is a servant in the Wicked Prince's palace, and when she saw I was leaving the city, she tried to make me go back with her. I was afraid she *would* make me, for she was tall and strong; but I would not listen to what she said, and at last she told me I was a stupid boy, and not worth speaking to."

Christian remembered how he had met with young Worldly at the same place, and he said, "You must be very glad you did not listen to her. Did you meet anyone else?"

"Not for some time. When I came to the Hill Difficulty, I saw a very old man sitting by the side of the road. He asked me whether I was going to the Heavenly City, and he said I had much better come and live with him, for he would be generous to me, and when he died I could have all his riches. He was so pleasant that I could not help listening to him, and he almost persuaded me to go with him.

"Oh," cried Christian, "he would have taken you to the Wicked Prince!"

Faithful Tells the Story of His Pilgrimage

"Yes, I am sure he would. I was just ready to turn back, but I looked up and saw that he was smiling to himself. Then it came into my mind that perhaps he was one of the Wicked Prince's servants. So I said, 'I will not go.' Then he was very angry, and told me he would send someone after me to hurt me. However, I escaped from him and went up the hill."

"Did he send anyone after you?" asked Christian.

"Yes. Just when I was passing the shelter I heard someone coming quickly behind me. He said he was one of the King's servants, and had come to punish me for listening to the old man. His name was Justice, and I thought he would kill me with his rod, but a man came by with a gentle face, and He told Justice not to strike me. I did not know who it was at first, but when He was going up the hill I saw the marks upon His feet, and I am sure it must have been the Prince Himself—the King's Son!"

"I have heard about Justice," said Christian; "but my Book says that the Prince let Himself be punished instead of the pilgrims, to protect them from the punishment of Justice. Did you not see the palace at the top of the hill?"

"Yes, and the lions, too. They were asleep, and it was quite early, so I thought it was better to go on my way."

"Watchful told me he had seen you. I wish you had stayed at the palace! The people are so kind. Did you meet anyone in the valley?"

"I met Discontent there, and he was very tiresome indeed."

"You did not meet Apollyon?"

"No."

"*I* did," said Christian, "and he very nearly killed me!"

CHAPTER 24

Talkative

The boys went on, talking happily together, until they came to a part of the journey in which the Way of the King was wider than usual. Faithful happened to turn his head, and he saw that another boy was walking on the opposite side of the road. Faithful thought that he might be a pleasant companion, so he said, "Are you going to the Heavenly City?"

The boy answered, "Yes."

"Then let us walk together," said Faithful. "We are all travelling the same way."

"I shall like that very much," replied the boy, and he crossed over the road and began to talk with Faithful.

He had a great deal to say about the King and His servants and His laws, and Faithful felt quite pleased to have a new friend who knew so much.

Presently Faithful waited for Christian, who was walking a little way behind them, and whispered, "Do you not like him? I am sure he must be a very good pilgrim."

Christian smiled. "Don't you know who he is?" he asked.

"No," said Faithful; "I have not seen him before."

"Haven't you? Why, he still lives in our old city. His

name is Talkative. He often pretends to be a pilgrim, just for fun; but I did not know that he ever came as far as *this*."

"Is he a bad pilgrim, then?"

"I am afraid he does not love the King," said Christian; "but you will soon find out."

Then Faithful ran on again, and walked by the side of Talkative.

"Perhaps," thought the pilgrim, "he may not be quite so bad as Christian thinks, and we may be able to persuade him to go with us."

But the more the boy talked, the less Faithful liked him, and at last he became quite sure that they could never be friends. It was plain that Talkative knew very little that was true about the King; for although Talkative said how delightful it was to be the King's servant, Faithful could see that he had no real wish to enter the Heavenly City, and that he was only pretending to be a pilgrim for the sake of amusing himself.

Faithful listened quietly for some time, while his companion talked about the King's goodness, and then he said, "I suppose you are very careful to obey all the King's laws?"

Talkative blushed, for he knew he always did just what he liked, although he was very ready to tell his friends what the King had commanded *them* to do!

He felt annoyed with Faithful for asking him such a question, and answered crossly, "I don't see that it matters to you."

Talkative

"I think it *does* matter," replied Faithful. "If you talk so much about loving the King, you ought to serve Him very well indeed."

"How do you know that I don't serve Him?" returned Talkative.

"I am not sure," said Faithful; "but I am afraid you don't."

"I wonder what you have to do with correcting *me!*" cried Talkative, in an angry tone. "I am older than you are!"

"I didn't mean to correct you at all, but I was not sure if you were a real pilgrim."

"A real pilgrim! Of course I am! But I know exactly how it is. Christian told you a lot of stories about me when you ran back to speak to him, and I suppose you believe them all."

Faithful did not know what to say, for he could see that Talkative was very angry indeed, so he walked on quietly without speaking.

"I don't care at all," said Talkative, presently. "If you choose to believe bad things about me, it's your fault, not mine. But I think you are a very rude, disagreeable boy, and I don't wish to talk to you any more: you can just walk by yourself, and leave me to do as I like."

He seemed so angry that Faithful made no answer, but let him go on his way alone, and waited for Christian who soon came up to him.

"Never mind," said Christian, when he heard what had happened. "I am glad he has not stayed with us, for I don't think he would have done us any good!"

How pleased the boys were to see their friend once more!

CHAPTER 25

The Pilgrims Meet Evangelist

Soon after they had parted from Talkative, the two pilgrims came to a wide open piece of land. No trees grew upon it, and there were no flowers among the short, dry grass. The Way of the King went straight across, and as Christian looked in front he felt glad that he was not alone, for the path seemed long and dreary. With Faithful for a companion the time passed quickly, and towards the close of the afternoon the tired pilgrims were glad to find that the way ahead looked better.

In the distance the country appeared green and beautiful, and Christian hoped that they might soon come to another one of the King's houses, where they would be allowed to rest until the morning.

Presently Faithful thought he heard footsteps behind him, and looking back, he saw someone whose face seemed like that of an old friend.

He stood still for a minute, and then he cried out, "Oh, Christian, Christian! do you see who is coming after us?"

Christian turned also, and shouted out in excitement, "It is Evangelist!"

How pleased the boys were to see their friend once

more! Evangelist had much to hear, and he smiled at the eagerness with which the two young pilgrims told him of all that they had seen and done.

"The King has been very good to you," he said at length. "You have met with some enemies and some troubles, but He has helped you always, and He will help you still if you trust in Him."

"I am sure He will," said Christian.

Faithful held his hand tightly in Evangelist's, but he felt shy and half afraid to speak; but Evangelist knew that he loved and trusted the King with all his heart, and that he would be just as brave as Christian if the servants of the Wicked Prince were to attack him.

"Will you tell us more about the road?" asked Christian. "Will it be easier now, or are there some other dreadful places to pass through?"

Evangelist looked serious. "I came to meet you here," he answered, "because very soon you will reach the gates of a great city which belongs to the Wicked Prince. It is a beautiful city, full of all kinds of pleasant things. Many pilgrims, when they enter it, are tempted to stay there instead of going on with their journey. I do not wish you to be so foolish, so I have come to warn you about it."

"Why must we pass through it?" asked Faithful.

"The Wicked Prince ordered it to be built across the King's Way, so that pilgrims cannot possibly get to the Heavenly City without passing through the very middle of it."

"What shall we do, then?"

The Pilgrims Meet Evangelist

"You must walk quietly along the streets. Do not
stop to look at the beautiful things in the shops and in
the market, and do not let the children persuade you to
play with them. Sometimes the pilgrims are not much
troubled by the townspeople, and sometimes they are
treated very cruelly."

"Would they *kill* us, do you think?" asked Christian.

"They may, perhaps, put you in prison," replied
Evangelist; "and they have sometimes been evil
enough to kill people who would not serve their
Prince. But do not be afraid. If you do have to die there,
the King will send His angels, and they will carry you
at once to the Heavenly City, and you will have no
more trouble or pain for ever."

The sun was just setting when Evangelist bade the
two pilgrims good-bye, and before its light had faded
away they saw in the distance the walls and gates of a
great and strong city.

"Are you afraid?" asked Christian.

"Not *very* much," answered Faithful. "The King
will take care of us, and you have your good armour."

"Yes, but I do wish that you had stayed at the Palace
Beautiful. Then you would have had some armour, too."

"Never mind," said Faithful. "I shall keep close to
you, and if the people *do* kill me, there will be no more
enemies to fight!"

He now put his hand around Christian's arm, and
Christian thought of the King, and tried not to feel
frightened. But he was only a youngster, and as they
passed under the wide archway, and heard the heavy

gates close behind them, he whispered to Faithful, "I should like Evangelist to be taking hold of my hand now!"

And Faithful said, "Yes. Perhaps if we had asked him he would have gone through the city with us. What a pity we did not think of it!"

CHAPTER 26

Vanity Fair

The Wicked Prince hated the good King who ruled over the Heavenly City, and it made him very angry to see the pilgrims on their way from his country to that of the King. He had built this city, which was called Vanity Fair, just beyond the Dark Valley and the wilderness. He knew that when the pilgrims reached its gates they would be feeling tired and faint, and he hoped that it would then be easy to persuade them to stay there, instead of going farther on the King's Way.

So he filled the great city with everything that was pleasant and beautiful. It had broad streets and handsome houses, and the stalls in its market were covered with glittering wares. All day long the people were passing busily up and down. They wore fine clothes, and spent their whole time in pleasing themselves, and the Wicked Prince took care to give them plenty of things to enjoy, so that they might never have a moment to spare in which to think of the King whom they had forsaken.

After they had lived in Vanity Fair for a short time most of the pilgrims used to forget the King altogether, and when they saw other pilgrims passing on their way to the Heavenly City, they were quite ready to help the servants of the Wicked Prince in persuading the travellers to give up their journey.

It was dark when the two pilgrims entered the town, so they slept in a sheltered corner near the gate until the next morning.

As soon as the sun rose they began their walk through the city. They thought that if they started early, they might perhaps reach the opposite gate before the streets became crowded with people.

But Christian's bright armour, and the new clothes which Faithful wore, were not like those of the people in Vanity Fair: The pilgrims had only gone a short distance before they were noticed by some boys who were strolling idly about.

"There are two pilgrims!" they cried. "Let us go after them and stop them!"

Christian and Faithful could hear the boys running up behind them, but they did not look round.

"Don't let us take any notice," said Christian. "Perhaps they will not speak to us."

But when the boys came up, they all gathered closely round the young pilgrims and would not let them pass.

"Tell us where you have come from," said one.

"And who gave you that armour and those clothes?" cried another.

"Why don't you look at the shops?" asked a third. "Boys like you don't want swords and shields! You should sell them, and buy some of these beautiful things!"

Christian scarcely knew what to say, for the boys

The Pilgrims in Vanity Fair.

were all speaking at once, and he felt quite confused; but Faithful answered bravely, "We don't wish for any of your things—we are going to the Heavenly City."

Then the boys laughed rudely, and one of them pushed Faithful, so that he would have fallen if he had not been holding onto Christian.

By this time many other children had run towards them, and some older people stopped also to see what was the matter. Then one of the Wicked Prince's servants passed by, and when he saw Christian's shining helmet he knew that the boys must be pilgrims; so he pushed his way through the crowd, and seized them both by their shoulders.

"What are you doing?" he asked. "*Our* Prince does not allow children to quarrel in his streets."

"We are not quarrelling," said Christian. "We were walking along quite quietly."

"That is nonsense," replied the man. "You have caused all this crowd and disturbance. You must come with me."

"We are the King's pilgrims," said Faithful. "We are not disturbing anybody. We only wish to pass through the city."

"I don't know anything about the King's pilgrims," answered the man. "I can see that you are two foolish, troublesome boys, and you must be taken before the Governor."

So he led them both down the street to the Governor's house, and the children of the town followed, laughing and mocking at the pilgrims for whom they had made such trouble.

CHAPTER 27

The Pilgrims Suffer for the King

The Governor of the city was really one of the Wicked Prince's chief servants, and he hated the King and His pilgrims almost as much as his master did.

When Faithful and Christian were brought before him, he was quite glad to think that he had an excuse for hurting someone whom the King loved, and he said, "You are two very troublesome boys, and you must both be beaten. Afterwards you shall be shut up in the iron cage, so that the children of the town may see you, and know what will be done to *them* if they follow your example!"

It was no use for the pilgrims to say anything. Christian became frightened when he heard the Governor's cruel words, and Faithful's cheeks grew very white, but he whispered to Christian, "Evangelist said that they might hurt us, but if we die we shall go straight to the Heavenly City. I shall think of the King, because He is sure to help me."

A man came forward to beat them. Then Christian determined to be brave too, and he remembered the picture he had seen in the house of Interpreter, of the Good Shepherd, whose feet were torn and bleeding.

"The Good Shepherd is our Prince," thought Christian,

A crowd of noisy girls and boys gathered round.

The Pilgrims Suffer for the King

"and *He* did not mind the pain! I must not, either, because I am the King's servant, and it is written in my Book that the King's servants are to be like the Prince." So, although the strokes of the heavy rod made his back and arms feel terribly sore and bruised, he behaved like a brave soldier, and did not cry out at all.

The prison was a place in the middle of the market, with bars of iron in front of it, so that it looked like a cage for wild animals. After they had been beaten, the two pilgrims had chains fastened upon their hands and feet, and the man who had beaten them put them into the cage and left them there.

Christian and Faithful could not stand upright, for they were badly hurt and weak with pain, so they sat down together and each tried to comfort the other by retelling the King's promises.

"We knew that they could be cruel," said Faithful, "but it is for the King that we have been hurt. He will always be with us!"

When the people in the town heard that two of the King's pilgrims were lying in the cage, they were very eager to see them, and soon a crowd of noisy girls and boys, and men and women also, gathered round to stare at Faithful and Christian, and to mock them in their trouble.

The boys of Vanity Fair said all kinds of cruel things to upset the pilgrims and to make them displease the King by being hateful and angry with their enemies. But Christian and Faithful sat still, and neither of them gave a cross answer to anything that was said.

At last some of the boys, when they saw how patient the two pilgrims were, began to feel ashamed and they cried out, "Let them alone now! They have been beaten, and they have behaved bravely. Don't tease them any more."

But the other boys were cruel, and liked to see the pilgrims suffer. So they went on teasing them and laughing at them, until their companions grew angry, and before long there was a great disturbance in the market, for the boys who were sorry for the pilgrims began to fight with those who were teasing them.

The Governor was obliged to send his men to stop the fighting, and he ordered Christian and Faithful to be beaten once more, because he said the quarrel had been their fault. Then they were taken back to the cage, where they lay all night in great pain and distress.

CHAPTER 28

Faithful Ends His Pilgrimage

When the morning came, Christian and Faithful were taken to the Governor's Court. The judge sat every day, to try any prisoners who might be brought to him. He was an old man, with a hard and cruel face, and, like the Governor, he hated the King and all His pilgrims.

Christian and Faithful were brought before him with their hands chained, and he asked where they had come from and what they had been doing.

Then a boy named Envy, who had been one of the first to run after the pilgrims and make fun of them, rose up and began to answer the judge's questions. He said He had known Christian and Faithful when they were living in the City of Destruction, and that they were disobedient and quarrelsome, and did not honour the Wicked Prince who was the ruler of their country.

Two other boys followed Envy, and they agreed that what he had said was quite true. They also told the judge that they were afraid the pilgrims would do great harm to the children of Vanity Fair if they were set free, because they laughed at the treasures with which the Wicked Prince had filled the city, and said they were not worth having, and they pretended that they

119

Envy accuses Faithful.

Faithful Ends His Pilgrimage

knew of a finer city and another King, whose laws were better than those of the Wicked Prince!

There were twelve men sitting in the court, whose duty it was to listen to everything that was said about the prisoners, and then help the judge to decide whether they deserved punishment or not. These twelve men were called the jury. They were chosen from among the chief servants of the Wicked Prince, and were not likely to be kind or just to any of the King's pilgrims!

However, they always pretended to treat their prisoners fairly, so when Faithful asked if he might speak to them, the judge answered, "You ought to be put to death at once for all that you have done, but we will first hear what you have to say."

Christian wondered how it was that Faithful had become so brave. His face was pale, but he did not seem to be frightened, although the judge and the people in the court looked wicked and cruel. Christian afterwards knew that the King had helped make Faithful brave and strong, so that he was not afraid to speak out and say that he loved his King dearly, and would obey no one else.

When Faithful had spoken, the judge turned to the jury and said, "You have heard what Envy and his companions have told us about these boys, and Faithful does not deny it. He refuses to serve our Prince, and by the laws of our city he ought to be put to death."

Then the twelve men answered, "We can see that both these pilgrims are wicked, but Faithful is worse, because he is not ashamed to speak against our Prince. We think that he must be *killed,* but Christian can be taken back to prison!"

Christian's mind had been so troubled by all that had happened, that he scarcely understood what the jury were saying. When the soldiers of the Wicked Prince came in and led Faithful out of the court, he wondered where they were going. In a few minutes he too was taken into the market place, and there he saw his companion in the midst of those cruel men, who were beating him with sharp weapons.

"Oh, Faithful! Faithful!" he cried out, but Faithful did not answer. He was looking up into the sky, and his face was shining with a beautiful light.

Then Christian looked up also, and in the air, just above the place where Faithful was standing, he could see a band of angels, and he knew that they were waiting to carry his young friend home to the Heavenly City.

CHAPTER 29

Christian Leaves Vanity Fair

Christian knew that Faithful would be carried safely into the presence of the King, and as he thought of this he forgot for a moment that he was in Vanity Fair, surrounded by the servants of the Wicked Prince. Suddenly the people of the city gave a great shout of pleasure, because they loved to see a pilgrim punished, and their cry startled Christian, so that he turned once more to look at his friend.

But the King did not wish Christian to know how much poor Faithful was suffering. A mist seemed to pass before his eyes, and he cried out again, "Oh, Faithful! Faithful!" Then a strange feeling came over him, and he felt himself carried away into an open space where there were no soldiers, and no noisy, mocking crowd.

There he lay for some time, feeling too weak to move or speak; but presently he opened his eyes, and found that he was in a small room upon a low bed, and that a woman was bending over him. She was dressed like all the women in Vanity Fair, and although she did not appear unkind, her face had a strange look that made Christian cautious.

She was the wife of the man who kept the prison,

Young Christian's Pilgrimage

and when Christian had been carried from the market place by the soldier who had taken charge of him, she had been sorry for him. So she brought some water, and bathed his hands and face gently, and stayed by him until he revived.

"You poor child!" she said, presently. "You are too young to be a pilgrim. I should like to keep you here, and take care of you."

"You are very kind to me," he said, "but I could not stay. I am going to the King!"

"Ah!" replied the woman, "I was going to the King once, but the way was hard, and I have been very happy here in the city."

"You would be happier with the King," said Christian. "Faithful is gone—I saw the angels waiting for him; and if they ever let me out of this city, I shall travel as fast as I can to the end of my journey."

The woman bent down closely to Christian. "Faithful is dead," she whispered. "I was sorry when they told me, but they are not going to kill you."

"I don't think I would have minded," said Christian, "for then I should have gone straight to the Heavenly City, and now perhaps I shall be kept here always; or, if not, I shall have to go the rest of the way alone."

"They will only keep you here in the city for a few days," answered the woman. "Stay with me. I will be very kind to you."

But Christian shook his head. "I couldn't stay. I love the King, and I must go to him."

After a few days the keeper of the prison came and

124

Christian Leaves Vanity Fair

told him that the governor of the city had given an order for him to be set free, so Christian started once more on his journey. The woman was sorry to see him go, and as he left, she bade him think of her sometimes.

"I will tell the King how you have helped me," said Christian, "and perhaps some day you will be a pilgrim again. If I see you coming into the Heavenly City I shall know you."

He went quietly down the street, not feeling strong enough yet to walk quickly, and being very much afraid that the boys would run after him, as they had done before. But because Faithful had been put to death they were satisfied, and although they all laughed when Christian passed, they did not touch or harm him in any way.

He was just going through the great archway of the city gate when he heard someone running behind him, and he felt a hand upon his shoulder. For a moment he was frightened, thinking that his troubles were beginning again, but the boy who had stopped him looked frightened too, and said in a half-whisper, "Let me come with you. I don't want to stay *here* any longer!"

"Do you mean that you will be a pilgrim?" said Christian.

"Yes; I am called Hopeful, and I want to go with you; but wait until we are safely on the road, and then I will tell you all about it."

CHAPTER 30

By-ends

Christian left the city of Vanity Fair as fast as he could, and Hopeful kept close to him, but he seemed afraid to speak until they were some distance from the city.

Then he said, "Some of us were sorry, you know, because they killed Faithful. He was very brave, and I am sure he was good; and there are many people who say that they will not stay in the city much longer if such cruel things are done there. I was just passing the prison when they let you go, and I watched you leave. Then, when no one was looking, I ran after you. You don't mind me coming, do you?"

"Not if you really love the King," replied Christian. "I thought I should have to go the rest of the way by myself, and I shall be very glad indeed if you will come too."

"Yes, I will come," said Hopeful. "I wasn't happy, and I always meant to run away some day."

Christian was just beginning to ask how long Hopeful had been living in Vanity Fair when they caught up with another boy, who was strolling very slowly on the sunny side of the road. He came from a city not far from Vanity Fair. The people who lived in it called themselves the King's servants, and pretended to love him very much; but whenever the Wicked Prince or his servants came to see them they left off talking about the King, and behaved as if the Wicked Prince were their ruler! The Wicked Prince liked these people, and when he heard that any of them had become pilgrims he never tried to hinder them in their journey, because he knew that they would be sure to turn back again as soon as they met with the least difficulty or danger.

The boy, whose name was By-ends, joined Christian and Hopeful, and walked with them for a short time. He told them that all his relations and friends were very rich people; and he seemed proud of his high position, and inclined to look down on Christian and Hopeful.

"Isn't it a beautiful day?" said Hopeful, presently, for the sun was shining brightly, and the breeze was soft and pleasant.

"Yes," replied By-ends; "it is just right for travelling. But pilgrims from our city never start in the winter. We always choose clear summer weather for our journeys. It is foolish to tire yourself with struggling against wind and rain."

"There are storms even in the summer," said Christian.

"You needn't travel in them. If it began to rain I should creep under a thick bush until it was fine again."

Christian could not help smiling, but he answered, "I am sure good pilgrims never do that. We ought not to mind about the weather."

"Well, of course," said By-ends, "you can do as you like. We need not quarrel about it. If there is a storm, you can walk in it if you choose, but I shall *certainly* wait until it is over!"

Christian had read in his Book that it is unwise for pilgrims to travel with friends who are not the King's true servants, so he said, "I am afraid if you think in that way we shall not be good companions for you. We must go straight on, whether it is fine or stormy."

"Very well," answered By-ends. "You had better go on by yourselves. I was very happy before you came, and I'm sure I don't want you to stay with me!"

"It was a pity to upset him," said Christian, as he walked on with Hopeful, "but I don't see how we could help it. If we stayed with him, and there happened to be a storm, he might persuade us to turn back altogether."

By-ends had really been feeling rather lonely, and was very glad when Christian and Hopeful met with him; but he was too idle and fond of his own comfort to be willing to serve the King faithfully, as they wished to do. He put his hands in his pockets, and tried to look as if he did not care when they left him, although he felt almost inclined to run after them, and say that he did not mind about storms any more than they did.

"They are silly boys," he thought, "but their company would be better than none."

But before By-ends had made up his mind what to do, he heard shouts behind him, and turning round he saw three of his school friends calling to him to wait for them.

"Where are *you* off to?" they cried, as they came up to him.

"There wasn't anything particular to do at home," said By-ends, "so I thought I'd try being a pilgrim."

"We'll go with you. Who are those two boys in front? We saw you talking to them."

"Oh, they are pilgrims, too," replied By-ends, "but not *our* sort. They are servants of the King. I told them I should only travel while the weather kept fine; so they said I would have to stay by myself. I don't see the use of plodding over rough roads in wind and rain. You may just as well stop until the storm is over."

"Of course," said one of the boys; "but the King's servants are always like that, and if you don't exactly agree with everything they say, they won't have anything to do with you! However, what does it matter! Let them alone, and we shall be a nice little group, travelling all by ourselves!"

CHAPTER 31

Demas and the Silver Mine

By-ends and his friends walked on together, laughing and talking. Christian and Hopeful were not very far ahead, and presently the four boys ran and caught up with them, and began to ask them foolish questions.

They pretended that they wished to know whether some of the things which they were fond of doing were wrong, and likely to displease the King. They hoped that Christian would not be brave enough to answer them truthfully, because then they would be able to call him a coward. But although Christian was sometimes shy, he was not afraid to speak the truth. He was learning to love the King, and no fear of what these boys might do to him would have made him agree with By-ends and his friends.

He answered all their questions honestly, and at last they began to feel ashamed of themselves, and said no more. Christian was very glad when they left him, and he went on with Hopeful, while By-ends and his three companions dropped behind.

Very soon the two pilgrims came to a place where the pathway was smooth and easy; and just beyond they saw a small hill with an opening in its side, like the mouth of a cave. A boy was standing upon the hill, and

"Come up here and see this!"

Demas and the Silver Mine

when Christian and Hopeful passed by he called down to them, saying, "Come up here and see this!"

"What is it?" asked Christian.

"A mine of silver," said the boy. "It is full of rich treasure, and you can soon gather up enough to take with you on your journey."

"Oh," cried Hopeful, "let us go and look at it!"

But Christian pulled him back. "No, no!" he said; "it is not a safe place!" Then he called to the boy, whose name was Demas, and asked him if it was dangerous.

Demas knew quite well that it was very dangerous indeed; but he was a servant of the Wicked Prince, to whom the mine belonged, and he had been sent there on purpose to tempt the pilgrims by telling them of its rich store of silver; so he answered, "It is safe unless you are very careless."

But Christian turned away, saying to Hopeful, "We will not go. I am sure I have heard about it, and you see we could not reach it without leaving the Way of the King."

Then Demas cried, "If you will not come, you might at least wait for me, and I will go with you. I am a pilgrim too."

"I don't think you are one of the King's pilgrims," replied Christian, "or you would not try to delay us on our journey. We cannot wait for anybody."

So Demas said no more, but watched for By-ends and the other boys, who were not far behind. Hopeful turned round to see what they would do. They had no love for the King, and they did not care at all about the

Young Christian's Pilgrimage

Heavenly City to which they said they were going; so when they heard of the treasure hidden in the hillside they hurried eagerly to the mouth of the cave. Demas knew that people who went into it to dig for silver were nearly always either lost or killed there, but he told By-ends and his friends that it was quite safe, and they were ready to believe everything that he said.

Christian and Hopeful saw them enter the cave, but no one ever heard anything of them again. They ventured too far along the dark and winding passages, and were never able to find their way back into the daylight.

When Christian and Hopeful had walked for some distance beyond the hill, Hopeful stopped suddenly, saying, "Oh, what can that be?"

Christian looked where he pointed, and saw a strange white figure standing by the roadside. As they came nearer, the boys saw that it did not move, and that it was in the shape of a woman, with her face turned away from the Heavenly City.

"Do you think she was a pilgrim?" whispered Hopeful.

"I don't know," said Christian. "It looks like a statue. I wonder why it is placed here by the wayside."

They walked round it, and looked at it carefully, and at last Hopeful saw a few words carved upon the border of the woman's veil, just where it lay upon her forehead. They were old and worn, and he could not make them out; but after puzzling over them a little, Christian read—

Demas and the Silver Mine

"Remember Lot's Wife."

"I know what it is," he said. "I read about it in the library at the Palace Beautiful."

Then he told Hopeful how the King had once rescued a man named Lot, with his wife and two daughters, from a city which was being destroyed for its wickedness.

"He sent an angel to bring them out, and the angel told them not to look back; but Lot's wife *did* look back, and the moment she turned, she became a pillar of salt, so that she could never move again."

"What a dreadful thing!" said Hopeful. "Is it put here to frighten us?"

"Not to frighten us, I think, but to make us careful. I am very glad we did *not* go up the hill when Demas called us!"

"So am I; for I should not like the King to be angry with *me.*"

CHAPTER 32

The Valley of Peace

The two boys were obliged to travel very slowly that day, on account of Christian's injuries received at Vanity Fair.

"Where shall we sleep?" asked Hopeful. "You cannot walk all night, and it will not be safe to lie down here by the wayside."

"Perhaps there is another house like the Palace Beautiful," replied Christian. "I *was* happy there! You cannot imagine how kind Discretion and her daughters were to me."

Then Hopeful began to ask questions about them, and Christian tried to tell him of all that he had seen and heard at the palace. But Christian's strength was failing after the day's journey, and he soon became too tired to speak, and could scarcely walk, even with the help of Hopeful's arm. Hopeful did all he could to cheer his weary companion; but he began to feel very anxious when he saw that Christian's face was growing paler every minute.

"If we could only find a place to rest in," he thought; and as the evening shadows closed round the pathway he strained his eyes eagerly in the hope of seeing some distant light, which would tell him that they were coming near to a house where they could stay until the morning.

But no light appeared, and presently the night came on, and still the two pilgrims crept slowly along, for Christian would not lie down upon the grass, even though Hopeful promised to watch carefully by his side.

"We will go on," said Christian. "I don't think the King will forget us. *He* knows how tired we are, and He will be sure to give us a place to rest soon."

By now the stars had begun to twinkle in the dark sky, and the moon rose over the hills and shed soft blue light upon the Way of the King. As Hopeful looked forward, he saw that the pathway was widening, and that a broad river was flowing in the distance.

"We are coming to a beautiful country!" he exclaimed. "Look, Christian! The river is close to the wayside, and the path must lead through that meadow, which is all fenced in and safe."

Christian looked, and the sight of the river and the thought of rest and safety revived him a little. In a short time they reached the brink of the water, and found that Hopeful was right. The Way of the King ran close to the river, which was called the River of Life, and the ground on both sides of it was protected by strong fences. There was a beautiful meadow, covered with soft grass and flowers, and shaded by tall, spreading trees, under whose branches the King's pilgrims could rest safely and have no fear of enemies.

Christian was thankful to lay his aching body upon a

The Valley of Peace

mossy bank. Hopeful sat by him, and watched the moonlight playing peacefully upon the rippling water. Soon he took Christian by the hand, saying, "The Wicked Prince never comes *here!*"

"Oh, no!" said Christian, "I am sure he does not. It is all so still and peaceful!"

The two pilgrims lay down and slept quietly until the morning. When the sun rose, a messenger came to them from the King.

"This is the Valley of Peace," he said. "You are to stay here for a few days, until Christian grows strong again. You will find plenty of food, for the trees are full of good fruit; and you must drink the water of the river, which will strengthen and refresh you."

So the boys spent a whole week in the Valley of Peace, resting and enjoying their life more and more every day. Christian was not afraid to loosen his armour in this quiet spot, and he used to sit by the river, leaning comfortably against the trunk of some wide-spreading tree, while Hopeful lay on the grass near to him, gathering up the delicious fruit which was now ripe and falling from the heavily laden trees.

After all Christian's troubles, the Valley of Peace seemed very pleasant; and soon the strength came back to his limbs, and he felt able to continue his journey.

"I don't think we are *very* far from the Heavenly City," he said, "and I shall be *so* glad when we get there! After this good rest we shall be able to travel faster."

CHAPTER 33

Two-path Corner

The pilgrims left the Valley of Peace early in the morning, and travelled along the Way of the King all that day. Late in the afternoon they came to a place where a stile led off into a broad, green meadow. It was called Two-path Corner, and the meadow belonged to a cruel and powerful giant named Despair. He was one of the most famous soldiers in the Wicked Prince's army. He lived in a strong castle beyond the meadow, which could not be seen from the Way of the King. This was all written in Christian's Book, but he did not think of looking at it just then.

The boys were both feeling very tired. They had found that the path leading from the river was rough and stony, and their feet were sore and aching.

Christian stopped when he saw the stile, and leaned over it. A fence divided the meadow from the Way of the King, but a smooth grassy path ran close to it.

"Could we not walk along this path for a little way?" he asked, turning to Hopeful. "These stones are so hard, and my feet ache dreadfully."

"So do mine," answered Hopeful; "but would it be safe?" Then he came to the stile also, and looked over.

"Oh, I think it must be safe," said Christian. "See, it

runs close to the fence. We could climb back onto this path again anywhere in a minute."

Hopeful did not feel quite sure that they were doing right; but as he thought that Christian knew more about the King's laws than he did, he followed his companion into the meadow. The grass was soft and pleasant to their feet, and not far in front of them another boy was walking near to the fence.

Christian called to him, saying, "Can you tell us where this path leads?"

The boy, whose name was Vain-Confidence, turned round and replied, "To the Heavenly City."

"You see," said Christian, "I was right. We shall be quite safe. We can keep behind that boy, and then if there *is* any danger we shall know of it in time to escape!"

But Hopeful was not satisfied, and when the night came on and the shadows grew so thick that the figure of Vain-Confidence could no longer be seen, he felt frightened. Suddenly a cry was heard, and a sound of falling. Hopeful seized Christian's arm, and clung to him in great fear; and Christian too lost his courage, and began to shake from head to foot.

"What can have happened?" he asked, and he called again to Vain-Confidence; but he received no answer, although through the darkness the boys could hear that someone was groaning as if in terrible pain.

"I am *sure* we are not in the right way," said Hopeful, "and it is *so* dark!"

Christian did not answer. He knew now that he had

Two-path Corner

done wrong in climbing over the stile, and he wondered how he could have been so foolish as to think that any path could be safe which led him out of the straight road.

Then, before he could speak again, he felt some heavy drops of rain upon his face. A bright flash of lightning darted across the sky, and a roar of thunder followed. The rain poured in torrents, and the thunder and lightning were more fearful than any which they had heard or seen before.

Christian began to wish that he had not been so careless. "It was all my fault," he said. "Oh, Hopeful, I am sorry! *I* deserve to be in this danger, but *you* would never have come if I had not persuaded you!"

"I might have done," said Hopeful, not liking to blame Christian. "It was my fault too, because I didn't try to prevent you coming."

"Let us turn back," said Christian. "Perhaps we can still find our way."

By this time the heavy rain had filled the streams which ran through the meadow, and the path by the fence was flooded. The water was so deep that the boys could scarcely keep their footing, and they began to fear that they would never get back into the Way of the King.

The storm lasted for many hours, and although Christian and Hopeful struggled bravely they soon found that it would not be possible to make their way back to the stile in the darkness. So at last they sat down together in a sheltered corner close to the fence,

Young Christian's Pilgrimage

meaning to stay awake and watch for the first gleam of daylight, and then hasten on their way. But they were both worn out with fright and weariness, and before the morning came they fell asleep.

CHAPTER 34

Seized by the Giant

The storm passed away before daybreak, and the sun rose in a clear sky, and shone brightly over the Way of the King. Christian and Hopeful were lying under the shadow of the fence, and did not feel the warmth of the sun, so instead of making their way back to the stile in the early morning as they had intended to do, they slept soundly, and knew nothing of the danger which was close at hand.

Giant Despair had heard the storm raging, and he came down from his castle soon after sunrise, and walked through his fields and meadows to see if any harm had been done by the wind and rain. Last of all he crossed his meadow, and on his way home passed by the very spot where the two pilgrims were sleeping.

Hopeful's clothes, which had once been so clean and new, had become dirty and shabby while he stayed in Vanity Fair; but Christian's armour still looked bright, although it was sadly splashed with the mud he had walked through the night before. The Giant caught sight of his shining helmet amongst the bushes by the fence, and he turned at once to see who was lying there.

"They are pilgrims of the King," he said to himself, and he smiled to think that they were in his power.

Young Christian's Pilgrimage

A loud voice roused Christian from his dreams, and when he opened his eyes he saw Giant Despair stooping over him. The Giant was a terrible-looking sight, with shaggy hair and beard, and clothes made of the rough skins of wild beasts. Christian cried out with fear when he saw him, and this woke Hopeful who sprang up in alarm.

"What are you doing here?" demanded the Giant.

"We are pilgrims," answered Christian, who was so afraid that he could scarcely speak; "and we have lost our way."

"You have no right to sleep in my meadow," said the Giant, and his voice was so harsh and deep that the boys were more frightened by it than they had been by the storm. "I shall take you back with me to my castle."

The two pilgrims knew that they were quite helpless. If they tried to run away this strong Giant would catch them in a moment. He led them across the fields to his house, which was called Doubting Castle, and put them into a dark dungeon, locking the door behind him.

All day and all night they lay there upon the bare ground, without either food or water, and not even able to see each other. Hopeful crept close to Christian and they sat together. Christian felt that he had caused all this trouble; and now he feared that the Giant would lock them up for ever, and that they would never reach the Heavenly City.

Giant Despair had a wife, whose name was Diffidence, which means "never sure." He told her that he found the two young pilgrims sleeping in his meadow, and that he had brought them home and locked them up in one of his dungeons. Diffidence was very pleased to hear this, and being a cruel woman she said that she hoped her husband would beat his two prisoners. So in the morning the Giant took a stick and went down to the dungeon.

When he had beaten the boys, he left them again in the darkness, and they were so bruised by the heavy blows that they could not move, but lay upon the ground all that day, twisting and turning with pain.

The next day Despair visited them again, and seemed surprised to find that they were not dead. He told them that he would never let them leave his castle, but that if they did *not* wish to die by starving to death, they could drink some poison which he would leave with them!

Then Christian begged him to have mercy upon them, and to set them free; and this made the Giant so angry that he rushed upon them with his club and would have killed them, but his strength suddenly failed, and he was unable to attack them that time. In the bright weather he often had fits of weakness, and lost the use of his hands, so that sometimes the pilgrims whom he carried into his castle were able to escape from him.

Christian did not know this, and he began to think that it was now foolish to hope for escape.

"What shall we do?" he asked Hopeful. "If we are to be kept here until we die, will it not be better to drink this poison than to die slowly for want of food?"

147

Young Christian's Pilgrimage

"I am sure we must not do that," said Hopeful. "If we were to kill ourselves, perhaps the angels would not come to take us to the Heavenly City. They only come when the King sends them. If the Giant is ill again, he may forget to lock the door, and we can then slip out before his strength comes back. Let us wait a little longer, and the King may show us a way to escape."

CHAPTER 35

The Key of Promise

In the evening, the Giant came down into the dungeon again, hoping to find that his prisoners were dead. But although they were very weak, they were still alive, and they had not touched the poison which he had left with them. This made Despair very angry, and he frightened the two pilgrims so much with his terrible looks and words that Christian hid himself in a corner of the dungeon. When at last he looked around, the Giant was gone, and only Hopeful sat by him.

"I think we shall have to take the poison," Christian said. "It is dreadful here; we cannot bear it much longer; and we shall never be able to escape."

"You must not talk in that way," replied Hopeful. "You are forgetting all the things that have happened to you before. Just remember what a long way you have travelled, and how many dangers you have been in. You were not afraid to fight with Apollyon, and the King helped you to conquer him. You passed safely through the Dark Valley, and even in Vanity Fair the King did not let you be killed. Let us trust in Him and wait a little longer."

The Giant came again and saw that the pilgrims were still alive, and when Diffidence heard this, she was no less angry than her husband.

"You had better take them into the courtyard tomorrow," she said, "and let them see some bones, and say that they belong to pilgrims who had died here before. Then perhaps they will be frightened, and will drink the poison. If not, you can put their eyes out so they will never see again!"

The Giant thought that this would be a good plan, and in the morning he brought Christian and Hopeful out of the dungeon, and led them into the courtyard, which he had covered over with bones. It was a very dreadful sight, and the Giant was pleased to see how frightened his prisoners looked. "These are the bones of pilgrims," he said. "They came into my meadow, as you did, and I brought them to my castle. In a few days your bones will lie here with the rest!"

Then he beat them once more, and they lay all day in their dark prison, wondering whether their troubles would ever come to an end.

The same night, when Despair was talking to his wife, he said that he could not understand how it was that these two boys were so very brave.

"Perhaps," replied Diffidence, "they think that someone will come to save them, or they may have a key hidden in their clothes, with which they will open the doors when we are not watching. You have lost prisoners in that way many times!"

This was quite true, but the Giant thought that if Christian had had one of the King's keys with him he would have used it before. "But I will search them both

The Key of Promise

in the morning," he said; and then he fell asleep.
Unknown to Christian, the key which was called the
Key of Promise lay in his pocket. It had been given to
him at the Palace Beautiful, but in his trouble he had
forgotten all about it.

Neither he nor Hopeful could sleep that night, and
after talking together for some time they began to pray
to the King, and beg Him to help them.

"He will hear us," said Christian, "though we cannot
see Him. I am beginning to feel that we shall escape
after all!"

The King heard the pilgrims' prayer, and He told
them what to do. They did not see Him, but a thought
came suddenly into Christian's mind, and that thought
was really the whisper of the King.

"Oh, how stupid I have been!" he cried. "We have
stayed here all these days, when we could have got
away at once! Discretion gave me a key, called the Key
of Promise, and I believe it will open every one of the
Giant's locks!"

Hopeful sprang up. "Let us try it!" he said. "It must
still be night, and no doubt Despair is asleep!"

They felt carefully in the darkness, until they found
the lock of the dungeon-door, and Christian put the key
into it. It turned quite easily, and with beating hearts
the boys stepped softly over the threshold and listened.

A dim light shone down the passage and they soon
found their way to the door which led into the
courtyard. This Christian opened also, and not daring
even to whisper, Hopeful followed. The moon was

Giant Despair.

The Key of Promise

shining brightly, and only one more door stood between the two pilgrims and the green meadow.

But this last lock was very stiff, and although Christian tried with all his might he could not turn the key. Then the Giant's step sounded upon the castle stairs, for he had heard someone moving. The boys thought that he would catch them, but just as Despair reached the doorway his club dropped from his hands, and he fell heavily upon the ground.

"Oh, *do* try harder!" cried Hopeful, "and we shall get away before he gets up!"

"I *am* trying," said Christian, "but the lock is rusty."

Hopeful put his hands also upon the Key of Promise. "It is moving!" he said, and in another moment the lock gave way.

The Giant still lay upon tne ground, and the boys hastily pulled back the heavy bolts, and opened the door. Then Hopeful seized Christian's hand, and they ran as fast as they could, across the broad meadow towards the stile which led into the Way of the King.

CHAPTER 36

The Delectable Mountains

"Oh," exclaimed Christian, when at last the boys found themselves once more on the Way of the King, "how glad I am that Discretion gave me the key!"

"Yes," said Hopeful; "what *should* we have done without it? When I held that key, I thought of all the promises the King has made in his Book."

They sat down together upon the roadside, for they were out of breath with running. They were not afraid to rest there, for they felt sure that Despair would not follow them into the King's Way.

"It is a pity that pilgrims do not know where that path will lead them," said Christian. "Could we not write something upon a stone, and set it up near the stile?"

"We can try," replied Hopeful. "I can make a warning sign, if we can find a stone."

They looked up and down, and presently they found a large, smooth block of stone lying amongst the grass.

"This will do very well," said Christian. "You mark out the letters first, and then I think we can push it into the right place."

So Hopeful drew out his knife, and carved these words upon the stone:—

Young Christian's Pilgrimage

"This path leads to Doubting Castle, which belongs to Giant Despair. He is the King's enemy, and he tries to capture pilgrims, but the Key of Promise opens all his locks."

Hopeful was some time over his task, but at last it was finished. Before the moon went down, the stone was pushed across the grass, and placed close to the stile, so that no one could pass by without seeing it.

"It will perhaps save someone," said Hopeful. "It was a good thing that you thought of it."

The short summer night was soon over, and the sun rose behind the hills. The young pilgrims walked on quietly, enjoying the daylight and the fresh air very much after spending those terrible days and nights in the dungeon.

"What beautiful hills those are!" said Hopeful; "and the Way of the King leads over them."

"I think they must be the Delectable Mountains," replied Christian. "I saw them far away, when I was at the Palace Beautiful. I believe some Shepherds live there who help pilgrims. Perhaps they will give us some food, and let us rest awhile."

Very soon the two pilgrims came close to the mountains, and began to climb the pathway which led across them. It was not steep and rugged like that upon the Hill Difficulty. It was smooth and easy, and the slopes on each side of it were planted with vines. Streams of pure water sparkled amongst the grass, and trees laden with fruit grew here and there, with

156

The Delectable Mountains

spreading branches which hung over the Way of the King, and sheltered the pilgrims from the heat of the sun.

Christian and Hopeful were very hungry, and thirsty also, and they were glad to eat some of the fruit, and to take a drink of the cool, clear water.

The Shepherds were not far from the path, and when they saw the boys coming, four of their number went down the green slope to meet them.

"Are these the Delectable Mountains?" asked Christian.

"Yes," replied one of the Shepherds. "This country is called Emmanuel's Land. It belongs to the Prince, and it is in sight of the King's City. These sheep are His, and we live upon the mountains to take care of them."

"Is it very far to the Heavenly City?" asked Christian; "and is the way safe?"

"It is safe for those who love the King, but pilgrims who do not serve Him faithfully can fall into danger."

"Is there any place here for pilgrims to rest?" asked Christian; "we are both so *very* tired."

"Oh, yes!" replied the Shepherds. "The King has commanded us to do all that we can for any of His servants who pass over the mountains. Come to our tents, and we will take good care of you."

So the Shepherds, whose names were Knowledge, Experience, Watchful, and Sincere, led Christian and Hopeful over to their tents. They brought them water to wash in and gave them plenty of good, nourishing

Young Christian's Pilgrimage

food. Then, seeing how tired the two young pilgrims were, Watchful prepared beds for them, where they slept comfortably and awoke early in the morning feeling refreshed and strengthened.

CHAPTER 37

The Rock of Error and Mount Caution

The next day, when the two boys were preparing to continue their journey, the Shepherds came to them and asked whether they would like to go for a walk upon the mountains before they left.

Christian and Hopeful thought they would enjoy this very much; so the Shepherds went with them over the broad, green slopes, and along the paths which had been cut upon the sides of the hills.

"It is not safe," said Knowledge, "for strangers to walk across these mountains alone, but the King allows us to take some of His pilgrims to see the view of the Heavenly City."

Presently they came to a steep path which was rugged and not very easy to climb. It led to the top of a great rock, and when they reached the highest point, Christian and Hopeful were glad to put their hands into those of the Shepherds, and hold on tightly. The rock was just at the edge of the mountain, and when the two pilgrims looked down from it they could see a valley far below.

"Do pilgrims ever fall from this rock?" Hopeful asked.

"Yes," replied the Shepherds. "This is the Rock of

159

Young Christian's Pilgrimage

Error. Pilgrims who leave the Way of the King, and wander upon the mountains alone, are fond of climbing up this pathway because they think they will have a better view from the rock. But when they look over, the sight of the deep valley makes them unsteady and sometimes they fall."

Then the Shepherds took the boys to another place, which was called Mount Caution. From it they looked upon a wide plain, where men, women and children were walking up and down. But they walked in a strange way, stretching out their hands as if to feel what was before them, and Christian noticed that they kept stumbling upon the rocks.

"Are they blind?" he asked. Experience answered that they were.

"Did you see a stile on the left-hand side of the road, not very far from these mountains?" asked Watchful.

"Yes," replied Christian.

"Beyond that stile is a path which leads to a strong castle. In the castle lives a giant named Despair. Many pilgrims go over into his meadow, because near to the stile the Way of the King is rough and stony, and the Giant's path looks green and smooth. Then they almost always lose their way, and Despair seizes them and carries them to his castle. He is very cruel to them; and often he makes them blind and brings them down to this plain, where they wander unable to continue their journey."

Christian and Hopeful looked at each other, but they did not speak. Perhaps, if they had not escaped from

The Rock of Error and Mount Caution

Doubting Castle with the help of the Key of Promise, they too would have been left to wander blind upon the plain!

The Shepherds now went down the mountains, on the side which was farthest from the Way of the King. Soon they came to a spot which reminded Christian of the entrance to the Dark Valley. Great black rocks were high above the path, and the two pilgrims could only see a very little distance down the narrow road because of a thick mist which lay before them.

"This is another dangerous place," said Knowledge, "but few pilgrims who walk upon the mountains are lost here. That dark path leads into the country of the Wicked Prince, and pilgrims who enter it are never able to find their way back again."

All these things made both pilgrims very thoughtful; but Christian said afterwards, "I am glad that we saw them, although I was frightened, because now we shall be very careful indeed about keeping in the Way of the King."

Far in the distance a beautiful light was shining.

CHAPTER 38

Ignorance

Last of all, the Shepherds brought the two pilgrims to the top of a high hill, called Mount Clear, from which they could see a very long way indeed. Far in the distance a beautiful light was shining, which dazzled their eyes when they tried to look at it.

"Where you see that light," said a Shepherd, "is the Heavenly City. If your eyes are good you will be able to see its gates."

But the light was brighter than that of the sun at midday, and its glory was too great for human eyes to bear.

"I can only see it shining," said Christian.

"It is too bright for you," said Sincere, "but we have a glass called Faith, which will make it seem clearer."

Christian took the glass, but the thought of the King's City, which he had so longed to see, made him tremble, and his hand shook so much that he could not hold the glass steadily.

Then Hopeful tried. "It dazzles me," he said; "but I think I can see something like a gate."

The walk upon the mountains had taken up the whole of the morning, so the Shepherds led the boys back to the tents, and made them rest awhile.

Young Christian's Pilgrimage

"When you have travelled a little farther," said Experience, "you will very likely meet a man called the Flatterer. He will try to lead you out of the Way of the King by praising you and saying wonderful things about you, but you must not listen to what he says."

Then Watchful told them that they would soon come to a place called the Enchanted Ground, where the air made pilgrims feel very sleepy. "It is a part of the Wicked Prince's country, and if his servants find you sleeping there, they will carry you away!"

"We will give you this map," said Knowledge, putting a sheet of paper into Christian's hand. "All the places you have to pass are marked upon it, and if you look at it carefully, you will not lose your way."

As Christian and Hopeful went down the mountain path, they talked together of all that the Shepherds had shown them.

"If we could only have seen the Heavenly City," said Christian, "I should have been so glad."

"Well," replied Hopeful, "we did see the glory of it, and we know that now it is not *very* far away."

At the foot of the mountain the boys came to a twisting lane. This lane led from a country called Pride, and a boy was running along it towards the Way of the King.

"Where have you come from?" asked Christian in surprise.

"From the country beyond the hills," he replied, "and I am going to the Heavenly City."

"But do you think they will let you in?" asked Christian.

Ignorance

"Why not? They let everybody in!"

"Not everybody. We have our Rolls of Faith to show that our names are already written in the Heavenly City. Did the King send you one?"

"No, but I don't suppose that will matter. I am His servant, because I always do what He bids me. I have heard that He wishes people to leave their own lands and travel to His city, so I am going, just as you are."

"But," said Christian, "the King's pilgrims ought to come in at the Gate, and pass by the Cross. Then they are given new clothes and a Roll of Faith. I am afraid you didn't do that."

"You needn't make such a fuss about it," replied the boy, whose name was Ignorance. "I don't know where you come from, but very likely you were living near to the Gate, and of course it was easy for *you* to enter by it! Nobody in my city ever thinks of going to it; in fact, I don't believe that anybody knows the way! We live in the city of Pride, and nobody tells *us* how to join the Way! We have that pleasant, green lane, which saves a lot of trouble, and makes *our* pilgrimage shorter!"

Christian scarcely knew what to answer, and as Ignorance stopped to gather some fruit, he and Hopeful passed on without him. He did not run after them, and Hopeful said, "Shall we wait for him?"

"I think not," replied Christian. "He will not want to be shown the true Way to the King!"

CHAPTER 39

The Story of Little Faith

Christian and Hopeful had not walked very far before they saw a band of soldiers in the distance. They were clothed in dark armour, which did not shine as Christian's did, and the pilgrims knew that they belonged to the army of the Wicked Prince.

"Do you think they will hurt us?" asked Hopeful.

"I don't know," replied Christian, and the boys both felt frightened, although they kept steadily on their way.

As the soldiers drew nearer, the children saw that they had a prisoner amongst them, and they knew by his clothes that he was one of the King's pilgrims. The soldiers were hurrying him along, and they took no notice of Christian and Hopeful as they passed by. The pilgrim hung down his head, for he was ashamed to let the boys see his face.

He had once loved the King, and he had travelled very nearly to the gates of the Heavenly City. Then he wandered from the straight path, and before long he met with some servants of the Wicked Prince, who pretended to be very kind to him. He stayed with them, and soon he forgot the good King, and left off obeying Him. He allowed his bright armour to grow rusty, and

167

his new clothes became dirty and ragged. His Roll of Faith was lost, and no one would have known that he had ever served the King at all.

But one day something reminded him of the Heavenly City, and he began to feel sorry, and wondered whether the King would forgive him. After a while he left his new friends, and tried to find his way back into the straight path.

The Wicked Prince heard that he was gone, and sent a band of soldiers to look for him, and when the poor pilgrim drew his sword to defend himself he found that it was spoiled with rust, and he could not use it. So the soldiers bound him with chains, and were now taking him back into the country of the Wicked Prince.

Christian and Hopeful were glad that the soldiers did not stop to speak to them, but they were also very sorry for the pilgrim, who seemed to be in great trouble. "We must ask the King to rescue the pilgrim," said Christian, and he and Hopeful fell to their knees and begged the King to send someone to release the man from the power of the Wicked Prince.

"I remember," said Christian, as they watched the soldiers go past, "when I was at the Palace Beautiful I read a story of a pilgrim named Little Faith, who was robbed not very far from this place. I think the Wicked Prince's servants often come here, and we must be very careful."

"Tell me about Little Faith," said Hopeful. "How was he robbed?"

"He was very tired," replied Christian, "and he sat

They threw him upon the ground.

down upon the grass to rest, and fell asleep. It was just at the corner of one of the lanes which we have passed, so it was not a safe place to sleep. Three boys (I think their names were Faint Heart, Mistrust, and Guilt) were playing in the lane, and they saw Little Faith lying at the corner, so they thought they would steal his things. He was just walking when they seized him and, before he had time to get his sword, they threw him upon the ground and beat him dreadfully. They took all the money out of his pockets, and then they thought they heard someone coming."

"Who was it?"

"There wasn't anyone really, but they knew they were doing wrong, and they were frightened. There is a little village called Good Confidence somewhere amongst these mountains, and one of the King's Captains lives there. The boys thought he had seen them, and so they ran away."

"And what became of Little Faith? Was he hurt very much?"

"Yes, but they had not stolen his Roll of Faith; so, although he was upset to lose his money, he felt comforted, and after a little while he was able to get up and go on his journey."

CHAPTER 40

The Flatterer and His Net

The boys were talking together about Little Faith and his troubles, when they came to a place where the road divided into two.

It was very difficult to see which path was the right one. When Christian and Hopeful stood on one side of the road, the right-hand path seemed to be straight, but when they crossed over to the other side, the left-hand path looked quite straight also.

"I don't know *which* is right!" said Christian, and they stood still to consider.

Now the Shepherds had given them a map, and if they had looked at it they would have seen at once which path to take; but instead of doing this, they began to waste their time by crossing the road from side to side, trying to find out for themselves which was the straighter of the two paths.

Presently a man came up behind them. His face was hard and unkind, but he wore a white robe, and the children supposed that he was a pilgrim.

"What is the matter?" he asked. "You seem to be very puzzled."

"Oh," replied Christian, "we are going to the King's City, and we cannot make out which of these paths is the right one!"

The man laughed. "Is that all?" he said. "You need not look so troubled about it. I am going to the Heavenly City myself. Follow me and I will show you the way. What clever, sensible young pilgrims you both are! Even if you have a map, you will not need it. You see, already you can tell that I am going the right way!"

So, without waiting to be sure that the man was really a pilgrim, Christian and Hopeful followed him. But very soon they discovered their mistake, for instead of going towards the Heavenly City, they found that they were going back to the Delectable Mountains.

"This path is not straight, I am sure!" whispered Christian.

Hopeful stopped at once. "Don't you think it is?" he said quietly.

"No. We ought to be going the other way. See, there are the hills where we were walking this morning. This path is leading us back to them."

"That man has deceived us," said Hopeful; "what shall we do?"

"We must turn back again."

"But perhaps he will run after us, and catch us. He cannot be a real pilgrim."

"I don't know," said Christian. "I wish we had not followed him! Let us run away."

The boys turned round hastily, but at that very moment the man turned also, and before they had time to take a single step towards the King's Way, they found themselves entangled in a large net which he

They struggled hard.

Young Christian's Pilgrimage

had thrown over them.

They fell upon the ground, crying aloud for help, but the man only laughed and walked away. Then his white robe slipped from his shoulders, and they realized that he was a servant of the Wicked Prince, and had dressed himself like a pilgrim in order to deceive anyone who would listen to him.

Christian and Hopeful struggled hard to free themselves from the net, but the more they pulled at it the tighter it became, and at last they were obliged to lie still, trapped together and thinking how foolish they had been.

"That man must be the Flatterer," said Christian, "and the Shepherds *told* us not to listen to him!"

"Yes," said Hopeful; "and we never looked at the map which they gave us, or we might have found out about the path at once."

"We are very bad pilgrims," sighed Christian. "We have gone the wrong way so many times. If only the King will save us just this once, I don't think we shall ever be so foolish again!"

CHAPTER 41

The Pilgrims Are Rescued

Christian and Hopeful began to fear that they would have to spend the night beneath the net of the Flatterer.

"And, perhaps," said Christian, "he has gone to tell the Wicked Prince, and he will send his soldiers to carry us away."

Just when the sun was setting, the pilgrims heard footsteps coming nearer and nearer, and even Hopeful could not help trembling. But only one man came in sight, and they knew by his shining garments and gentle face that he really was one of the King's true servants.

When he saw the two pilgrims he stopped. "How did you get into this net?" he asked.

"We were puzzled," said Christian, "and we could not make out which way to take. Then a man with a white robe came to us, and told us he was going to the Heavenly City, so we followed him."

"It was the Flatterer," said the King's servant; and then he stooped down and tore a large hole in the net. Christian and Hopeful were soon able to crawl out of it, and they stood upon the path before him, waiting for him to tell them what to do. His face was serious, and

Young Christian's Pilgrimage

Christian remembered how Evangelist had looked at him in the same way, when he found him wandering amongst the terrible rocks.

The King's servant turned towards the Way of the King, and told the boys to come after him. Christian took hold of Hopeful's arm, and they walked on together. When they were once more in the right path the King's servant stopped. "Where did you sleep last night?" he asked.

"With the Shepherds upon the mountains."

"Then where is your map of the Way?"

The boys hung down their heads, for they felt very much ashamed.

"Did you look at your map when you were puzzled?"

"No," whispered Hopeful; and Christian added, "We forgot."

"And what else did the Shepherds say to you? Did they warn you about the Flatterer?"

"They told us we were not to listen to him."

"And yet you *did* listen to him. How was that?"

"He told us that we were such clever and sensible pilgrims that we did not need to look at our map. We did not think that man *could* be the Flatterer, because he spoke so kindly to us."

The King's servant laid his hands upon the boys' shoulders, and spoke gently to them. "You have been very foolish," he said, "but I think you are sorry."

"We are very, very sorry," said Christian; "and it was more my fault than Hopeful's."

"No," said the King's servant, "you were *both*

The Pilgrims Are Rescued

wrong. If the King had not sent me to look for you, you might have been carried away by the soldiers of the Wicked Prince."

But, although the King had sent His servant to seek for the lost pilgrims, and to bring them back into the right path, He was not pleased with them, although He loved them very much.

"The King will forgive you," the servant said; "but you would not have lost your way if you had done as the Shepherds told you. You have learnt a lesson from your foolishness, and been punished for it. You have been pilgrims for a long time now, and should have known better than to go your own way."

Then the King's servant told them that the King would not remember their disobedience any more.

"Our Prince," he said, "was once a pilgrim Himself, and He has not forgotten the dangers and difficulties of the way. He is always watching over you, and when you are careless He begs His Father to forgive you, and His Father has promised that He always will."

CHAPTER 42

Unbelief

After the King's servant had left, the two pilgrims went steadily on their way. For two or three days they met with neither friends nor enemies. They were now crossing a very wide plain, which lay between the Delectable Mountains and a beautiful country with low hills and long valleys, which was marked upon their map as the "Land of Delight." Part of the plain was called the Enchanted Ground, and Hopeful reminded Christian that the Shepherds had warned them not to fall asleep there.

"I have not forgotten," said Christian, "but I am glad you remembered too. We must be very careful now, for after all this long journey it would be dreadful if we were carried away like that poor pilgrim we saw the other day."

"We will not listen to any more Flatterers," said Hopeful. As he said this, he held Christian by the arm. "Is that a man coming along the road towards us now?"

"Yes," replied Christian after stopping to look. "He is walking away from the Heavenly City. Look, he is coming to meet us!"

"He has pilgrim's clothes, but he is going the wrong way," said Hopeful.

Young Christian's Pilgrimage

The man, whose name was Unbelief, stopped when he met the children, and asked them where they were going. He had a pleasant face, and his voice was gentle, but the boys knew that they must not trust his words.

"We are going to the Heavenly City, the city of the King," said Christian, in answer to his question.

Unbelief laughed. "You poor fellows!" said he. "Have you really travelled all this long way without finding out the truth?"

"What truth?" asked Hopeful.

"It is such a tiresome journey," continued Unbelief, "and if you ever get to the end of it you will only be disappointed."

"Why?"

Then Unbelief pretended to look sad. "There is no King," he said, "and no Heavenly City."

"Oh, but there *is*," exclaimed Christian. "We have heard about it from the King's own servants!"

Unbelief put his hand upon the boy's shoulder and tried to turn him round. "My dear boy, you are young, and I am growing old. Listen to what I have to say. Long, long ago I heard the very same story which was told to you. I left my home and came to look for the King's City."

"Well," said Christian, "you will find it soon, will you not?"

"No," replied Unbelief. "I have been much farther than you have; I have spent twenty years as a pilgrim, and I can find no city at all."

Then Christian turned to Hopeful with a very

sorrowful face. "Do you think he is speaking the truth?"

"No," said Hopeful, "I am sure he is not! Do not listen to him! You know we *saw* the city from the Delectable Mountains. Let us make haste, or we may miss the path again."

Unbelief stood by, watching the two boys. "Come back with me," he said, "and I will take you safely to your own homes again."

But Christian answered him bravely. "You are trying to deceive us, but we do not believe what you say. We are quite sure that the King's word is true, and that there *is* a Heavenly City. We saw its gates when we were with the Shepherds!"

Unbelief shook his head. "You are mistaken, but you can go and look for it. I am going back to my own country."

"And *we* are going to the King!" replied Christian.

So they went on again, and Unbelief laughed at them as he turned away.

CHAPTER 43

The Enchanted Ground

They came, a little later in the day, to a part of the plain called the Enchanted Ground. It was a very pleasant place, so sheltered by the hills that the air was always soft and warm. The streams flowed gently along, the breeze scarcely stirred the leaves of the trees, and everything around seemed quiet and happy. But the meadows on either side of the Way of the King were not fenced in like those in the Valley of Peace, therefore it was not safe for pilgrims to lie down and rest in them.

The soldiers of the Wicked Prince were often hidden amongst the rocks and bushes, and when travellers were foolish enough to sleep there they were almost sure to be robbed, or even captured and carried away.

"Oh, dear," exclaimed Hopeful presently, "I am *so* sleepy! My eyes keep shutting every minute. Do let us sit down and rest for a little while."

"Not here!" said Christian, and he seized Hopeful's arm and shook him gently. "Hopeful! Hopeful! you are forgetting! This is the Enchanted Ground!"

"Well," replied Hopeful drowsily, "there is no one to hurt us. I will only stay a few minutes, Christian. Don't wait for me."

Young Christian's Pilgrimage

He threw himself down upon the grass; but Christian quickly pulled him up again, and this time he shook him violently.

"What *are* you thinking about?" he said. "Don't you remember what the Shepherds told us?" And he did not rest until Hopeful was thoroughly awakened.

Then Hopeful was frightened at the thought of his danger. "What *should* I have done if I had been alone! I am sure I should have fallen asleep. I have never felt so tired in all my life."

"I was just beginning to feel sleepy, too," replied Christian, "but shaking you helped to wake me up. We can be very thankful that we are travelling together. Let us talk about something interesting. That will keep us awake. You have never told me how it was that you began to be a pilgrim."

"I started before you did," said Hopeful. "I knew young Faithful very well, and when Evangelist first talked to him, Faithful used to come to me afterwards and tell me what he had heard about the King. I did not take much notice at first, but after a time I thought it would be nice to live in the Heavenly City. One day I ran off to the Gate and began my journey on the King's Way. But when I came to Vanity Fair I stopped to play in the streets, and at last the people there persuaded me not to go any farther; so I stayed."

"You didn't like it really, did you?"

"No. At least, I liked it sometimes, but often I used to feel frightened and unhappy. When pilgrims passed through the town I was ashamed, and afraid that they

The Enchanted Ground

would recognize me. Then you came with Faithful, and the minute I saw him I knew who he was."

"Did you see us beaten?" asked Christian.

"Yes, and I watched you when you were in the cage. Once I crept up close to the bars. I think you must have been asleep, but Faithful saw me, and he spoke to me."

"What did he say?"

"He begged me to leave the city at once, and he said the King would forgive me, because the Prince—His Son—loves us. Then I saw Faithful suffer because he loved the King, and I made up my mind that when you were set free, I would ask you to let me go with you."

"I am so glad you did," said Christian. "We have been very happy together. Don't you feel glad too?"

"Yes," replied Hopeful, "indeed I do! I am sure now that the King has always loved me, and it will not be very long before we are both safe in His beautiful city!"

CHAPTER 44

The Pilgrims Wait for Ignorance

All this time Ignorance had been travelling slowly along by himself. The Flatterer and Unbelief never took any notice of him, because they knew he had not begun his pilgrimage in the right way. They knew that when he reached the Heavenly City the King's servants would not allow him to enter its gates, but would send him back to his own master, the Wicked Prince. So Ignorance met with no trouble or difficulty, and did not even feel sleepy when he crossed the Enchanted Ground.

While Hopeful and Christian were passing over the Enchanted Ground they remembered Ignorance, and wondered how he was getting on. Presently Hopeful looked back.

"He is only a little way behind us," said he. "Shall we wait for him?"

"Perhaps it would be better," replied Christian; "then, if he feels sleepy, we can keep him awake."

The two pilgrims waited, but although Ignorance saw that they were standing still, he did not seem to care about catching up with them.

"It is a pity for you to stay behind," said Christian, as the boy came slowly towards them. "Won't you walk with us?"

Young Christian's Pilgrimage

"I don't care," replied Ignorance. "I would just as soon walk by myself. I always have so much to think about."

"What is it that you think of?" asked Hopeful.

"The King and the Heavenly City."

"But *thinking* about them is not enough," said Christian. "We ought to make *sure* we will *see* the King and his City!"

"I think I will see the King."

"Then why don't you travel faster?"

"I am travelling quite fast enough. I am sure that I shall reach the City some day, and why should I not take my journey comfortably?"

"But, perhaps if you are so careless about it, you will fall into trouble or danger."

"Well, if I do, the King will help me."

"The King will not help you if you do not belong to Him," said Hopeful, who felt sure that Ignorance did not really know much about the King.

"I *do* try to obey Him," answered the boy. "I have left my home and become a pilgrim. What else can I do?"

"You did not enter by the Prince's Gate, nor did you pass by the Cross," said Christian; "and I am afraid that if you have not a Roll of Faith, the King will not let you enter His City."

"I am sure you are quite wrong in what you say," replied Ignorance. "I have read that the Prince will give me all I need to be a pilgrim. Why should I travel past the Gate and the Cross? It would seem as if I was not good enough already to be a pilgrim!"

The Pilgrims Wait for Ignorance

Then Christian remembered the paper which Evangelist had given to him before he left home. Perhaps Ignorance had one like it. "Did the King send you a message?" he asked.

"A message? No, of course He did not! I should never expect a great King to send a message to a boy like me."

Christian felt quite puzzled. "I don't know what to say to him," he whispered to Hopeful. "I am sure he is wrong, but he will not believe us."

But Ignorance was now tired of talking. "I really can't keep up with you," he said; "you must go on by yourselves." And as the two pilgrims had nothing further to say to him, they went on and left him to follow as slowly as he wished.

189

CHAPTER 45

The Land of Delight

Christian and Hopeful, having passed over the Enchanted Ground, found themselves in the Land of Delight. It was the most beautiful country they had ever seen. Its mountains were covered with trees, and its valleys were green with soft grass and bright with the loveliest flowers. In the distance shone the glorious light which the Shepherds had shown them from the Delectable Mountains, and as the two pilgrims' eyes grew accustomed to its brightness they were able to distinguish the walls and gates of the Heavenly City.

The Wicked Prince and his soldiers never came into the Land of Delight. The people who lived there were all true servants of the King, and they received Christian and Hopeful very kindly.

"Your troubles are over now," they said. "You have only to stay here and be happy until the King sends for you."

"Will that be soon?" asked Christian.

"We cannot tell you that," replied the people. "Sometimes the pilgrims live quietly in this land for many years. Sometimes the King gives them work to do for Him in the country of the Wicked Prince, but at last they all go to the Heavenly City to live with Him for ever."

Young Christian's Pilgrimage

"I remember," said Christian, "when Help drew me out of the Slough of Despair. He said that he had been to the gates of the City, but the King had given him some work which he would have to do before he entered it."

And while Christian wandered up and down the mountains and along the beautiful valleys with Hopeful, he began to wonder how soon he would meet with his mother and with his friends in the Heavenly City.

"Oh it will be nice to see them all again! Perhaps some of them have heard that we are here, and may be watching for us even now!"

The two pilgrims spent many happy days in the Land of Delight, and one morning they came to a valley which was laid out in vineyards and large gardens. The gates were all wide open, and as the two friends stopped to look at the trees and flowers, one of the gardeners spoke to them.

"You need not stay outside," he said. "These are the King's gardens, and they are for pilgrims to walk in."

Then he led them about amongst the vines and flowers, and in the evening he showed them a quiet shelter where they could lie down and sleep safely.

"Oh," said Christian, as they sat watching the sun which was slowly sinking behind the hills, "don't you feel glad that we came? I seem to be forgetting all the troubles we have had, now that we are so happy."

"I am so thankful that I ran away from Vanity Fair," said Hopeful; "and it was such a good thing that I did not lose my Roll of Faith there. I don't know how it was that I managed to keep it safely. The King must surely have been helping me!"

"And now we have only to wait for the King's message," continued Christian. "I would go away and work if He wished it, but I think I would like best to go straight into the City."

"So would I," said Hopeful; and then they lay down in the safety of the shelter, and slept quietly until the morning.

CHAPTER 46

The Dark River

The Land of Delight was so very near to the Heavenly City, that the angels often came down to visit the people who lived there. Very often they brought messages from the King to His servants, and the pilgrims knew that some day a message would be given to them.

They slept one night in the shelter in the King's garden, and the next morning when they were walking slowly along among the vines, they saw two angels coming down the path to meet them.

"Are you travelling to the Heavenly City?" they asked.

"Yes," replied Christian and Hopeful.

Then the angels asked many questions, and Christian and Hopeful told them of all that had happened since they began their pilgrimage. Christian told of all his difficulties and dangers, and Hopeful told how he had wasted his time in Vanity Fair.

"We have often behaved badly," they said; "but we are really sorry, and we do love the King with all our hearts."

"He knows that you do," replied the angels, "and He has forgiven you for all your mistakes and disobedience because of the love of His Son. No one is good enough to earn this forgiveness; it is a free gift offered by the King, and He knows that you have accepted it. He has sent us now to tell you that He wishes you to enter into His City."

When Hopeful heard this, his heart was full of joy. Christian was glad also, but when he thought of going into the presence of the King he began to feel troubled, and he said to the angels, "Will you go with us?"

"We will go a little way with you," they said, "and we will meet you again at the gates of the City."

Then they desired the two pilgrims to follow them, and they all went together out of the garden and down to the shore of a very wide river. Its waters were dark and rough, but the light from the Heavenly City was shining brightly beyond it.

"Oh," cried Christian, "how are we to cross over?"

"You will have to walk through the water," replied the angels, "but you must not be afraid. The City is on the other side, and you will very soon be safe within its gates."

Hopeful raised his head, and looked across the river. On the opposite shore he could see the pathway winding up the hillside towards the glorious golden gates. "Oh, Christian!" he said, "we need not be frightened now! We are so *very* near to the City."

But Christian's eyes had grown dim with fear, and he could not see the light beyond the river. He shivered as he looked at the water, and then he turned once more to the angels. "It is deep!" he said. "We shall be

Through the Dark River.

drowned if we try to cross it!"

"No," replied the angels, "you will not find it too deep. You must not look at the water, you must lift up your eyes to the light, and the King will help you."

"Will you come with us?" asked Christian again, and Hopeful wondered why he looked so pale and frightened.

"We cannot come with you," replied the angels, "but we shall meet you on the other side, and lead you to the presence of the King."

"Do all pilgrims cross it safely?"

"Yes. Do not be afraid! Trust in the King, and remember all that He has done for you."

Then the angels turned away, and Hopeful put his arm round his companion's shoulders. "Come, Christian," he said, "this is our very last trouble, and it will soon be over. Let us go together, and I am sure the King will take care of us."

So the two pilgrims went slowly down the bank, and stepped into the water.

CHAPTER 47

Ignorance Crosses the River

When Ignorance entered the Land of Delight, the people who met him spoke kindly to him, as they had done to Christian and Hopeful; but they soon found out that he was not a true pilgrim, and that he did not care to talk with them, so they left him to himself.

Ignorance passed by the gates of the King's gardens, but the gardeners did not invite him to come in; and the angels, although they often watched him as he walked along, did not speak to him or give him any encouraging message from the King.

At last he came to the brink of the Dark River. He could see the walls of the Heavenly City on the other side, and he knew that his journey would not be ended until he had crossed the water. He stood for a few minutes wondering what he should do, and then he lay down on the grass.

"I will rest a little," he thought, "and perhaps someone else will be crossing presently. I do not see any bridge, so there must be a boat to carry the pilgrims over."

There was a boat, but it belonged to the Wicked Prince, and the King's pilgrims never used it. The boatman, whose name was Vain-Hope, soon saw

Ignorance lying upon the bank and rowed towards him.

"It is time for you to go over the river," he said. "I have brought my boat for you."

Ignorance was pleased, and he got up at once, saying, "I suppose the King sent you."

"Yes," replied the man. "The water is not very deep, and many pilgrims try to walk through it; but there is no need to do so, because I am always ready to take them over."

He held out his hand and Ignorance took it, and stepped down into the boat. Then Vain-Hope caught up his oars, and rowed quickly across the rough water.

"What shall I do now?" asked Ignorance, when he had climbed up the opposite bank.

Vain-Hope pointed to a path. "That is the best way," he said. "It is smooth and easy. If the King's angels had come to meet you, they would have taken you by another road which is steep and difficult to climb. Go straight up to the gate, and you will soon find your way to the King's palace."

He pushed his boat off from the shore, and Ignorance turned round and began to climb the hill towards the City. He did not meet anyone, and when he reached the gates he found that they were closed. He looked up and saw some words written upon the archway in letters of gold—

"HAPPY ARE THOSE WHO WASH THEIR ROBES CLEAN, AND SO HAVE THE RIGHT TO EAT THE FRUIT FROM THE TREE OF LIFE AND TO GO THROUGH THE GATES INTO THE CITY."

Ignorance Crosses the River

"Well," thought Ignorance, "I *have* tried to keep clean for the King always," and he knocked at the gate. He quite forgot that the King had said His pilgrims must begin their journey at the Gate, and must travel by the Way of the Cross. He had heard of this many times; but he had not bothered about it, and so the King's blessing could not be given to him. He knocked twice, but no one opened the gates. Presently one of the King's servants came to the top of the archway, and when he saw Ignorance he said, "Where do you come from, and why are you knocking at the King's gate?"

"I am a pilgrim," replied Ignorance. "I have just crossed the river, and I wish to live in the Heavenly City."

"I will take your Roll of Faith," said the King's servant, "and carry it to my Master."

Ignorance knew that he had never received a Roll, but he put his hand into the folds of his clothes, and pretended to feel for it. The King's servant waited a little while, but at last he said, "I am afraid you have come without one." Then he went down from the gates to ask the King what he should do.

Poor Ignorance stood outside, and now he began to wish that he had not been so careless about his journey. "The City is so beautiful," he thought; "I *should* like to have lived there always, and I am afraid they will not let me go in!"

When the King heard that a pilgrim had come to the gates, who had not come by the Way of the Cross, He said, "I do not know him. He must be sent away!"

Then two of the angels came quickly and carried Ignorance away from the Gates of the Heavenly City into the country of the Wicked Prince.

His cruel master rejoiced when he was brought back. "It was your own fault," the Wicked Prince said, when he found Ignorance crying bitterly at the thought of his lost happiness. "If you had really wished to live with the King, you should have joined the King's Way by doing as He told you. The King's own Son built the Gate, but you chose not to go through it!"

CHAPTER 48

The End of the Pilgrimage

Christian gripped his hands together as he felt the cold waters of the Dark River rushing round his body. Hopeful kept close to him, and tried to hold him up; but Christian soon lost his footing, and cried out, "I am sinking! The water is going over me!"

"No, it is only waves," said Hopeful. "Do not be so frightened. I can feel the ground at the bottom of the river, and it is quite firm. We shall cross safely, and then we shall have no more trouble."

"Perhaps *you* will cross," whispered Christian faintly, "but I am sure I cannot. I shall never see the King, and I did *so* wish to live with Him always!"

"You *will* live with Him! Look up, Christian, and don't think about the water! We can see everything quite clearly now. The City is full of light, and the angels are waiting for us at the gates."

"They are waiting for *you*," said Christian, "not for me!" Then his head sank down on Hopeful's shoulder, and for a little while he did not seem to hear anything that his companion said. But Hopeful held him tightly in his arms, and prayed very earnestly to the King to help them both in this last trouble.

Presently Christian opened his eyes, and as the light

203

from the Heavenly City fell upon his face he cried out suddenly, "Oh, I can see it all now! It shines like the sun, and I heard the voice of the Prince. He said, 'Whoever believes in the Son has eternal life.' "

"Then I am sure we need not be frightened," said Hopeful. "Take hold of my hand again; the Prince will *never* break His promise!"

So Christian's courage came back to him, and he was not afraid anymore. Hand in hand the two pilgrims made their way across the Dark River, and after a time its bed seemed to grow firmer, and its waters were less rough. Then they saw that the two angels who had brought them down to the river were waiting to receive them. In a few moments the crossing was over. Gentle hands drew them out of the water, and they stood safely upon the shore.

The Heavenly City was built upon a hill, and a broad, straight road led from the river to its gates. This road was steep, as Vain-Hope had said it would be when he pointed out the easier path to Ignorance; but Christian and Hopeful did not find it difficult, for the angels held their hands and took care that they did not slip.

"We shall soon be in the City now," said Christian, who had forgotten all his fear and sorrow, and could only look up at the bright walls and gates which rose before him.

"Yes," replied the angel with whom he was walking, "you will see the King and He will receive you as His own child."

"Will He really let me live in His City always?"

The End of the Pilgrimage

"Yes, and you will never be tired or sad any more. You will have work to do for the King, but it will be easy and pleasant, and you will love to do it."

"Shall I find my mother?" asked Christian; for in the midst of his happiness he remembered her, and longed for the time when he should see her.

"She is coming to meet you now," said the angel. "She knows that you are with us, and she is so glad that your pilgrimage is over, and that you have crossed the river safely."

CHAPTER 49

The Heavenly City

The two pilgrims were now very near to the City, and a band of the King's servants, who had been watching at the gate, came quickly down the steep path to meet them.

"These are two of the King's pilgrims," said the angels, "and we are bringing them home to the Heavenly City."

Then, as Christian looked up, his mother was standing before him, and her eyes shone as she watched him. Christian knew her in a moment, and he ran into her arms.

"I have come to you, I have come!" he cried. "The King has taken care of me, and some day I am sure He will bring my father too!"

"I shall never lose you again," said his mother. "The King is very good. Come with me into His City that we may thank Him together."

Although Hopeful had not any friends to welcome him, for he had left them all behind him in the City of Destruction, the people gathered round and spoke kindly to him and he forgot his loneliness.

Christian had left his armour by the side of the river, for he would never need to fight again. Now he looked

They blew their trumpets loudly.

down anxiously at his clothes. He had tried to take care of them, but he knew that they had become soiled and dusty during his long journey, and he feared that the King would be displeased when He saw them. But the waters of the Dark River had washed away all the dust and stains. Even Hopeful, whose clothes had been sadly spoiled while he stayed in Vanity Fair, found that his clothes looked as fresh and new as they did when he first received them.

Close to the walls of the Heavenly City a number of angels were standing, with silver trumpets in their hands. When Christian and Hopeful came up to them, they blew their trumpets loudly to let the people in the City know that some pilgrims were waiting to enter into the King's presence. Then the people told Christian and Hopeful to knock at the gates, and the King's servant looked down from the archway, and took the Rolls of Faith which they gave to him, and carried them to the Palace. The Rolls were sealed with the Prince's own seal, and when the King saw it He was glad, and told His servant to open the gates at once, and to bring both the pilgrims before Him.

The people of the City had heard the sound of the silver trumpets, and they all knew what it meant. When Christian and Hopeful passed through the gateway, they found young Faithful and a great crowd waiting to receive them with music and songs of welcome. Everyone looked glad and happy, for there was no sorrow in the Heavenly City, and no weariness, and no pain.

Young Christian's Pilgrimage

At first Christian's and Hopeful's eyes were dazzled by the golden light which shone around them but by degrees they grew accustomed to it and were able to look up. Before them, in the middle of the City, rose a very stately palace, far more glorious than the Palace Beautiful.

"Does the King live there?" whispered Christian to the people close to him.

"Yes," they replied; "and when you have knelt before Him and seen His glory, you will be perfectly happy for ever!"

"I am happy *now*," said Christian, "because I have found all of you, and you love me."

"Ah, yes," someone answered; "but the love of the King is far greater than ours."

The two pilgrims had now reached the threshold of the Palace, and as the doors were thrown open they heard a sound of the most beautiful music. The Prince Himself was waiting to receive them, and He smiled upon them, and took their hands in His own. "Do not be afraid," He said. "I am the first and the last. I am the living one! I was dead, but now I am alive for ever and ever." Then He led them into the Palace, and the whole City was filled with joy because their pilgrimage was over. They had been brought safely through the Dark River, and were now being taken into the presence of the King.

The prison on Bedford Bridge.

Bunyan's birthplace, Elstow.